The Secret Forest

Also available:

The Secret Island
The Secret of Spiggy H
The Secret F
The Secret of M

Enid Blyton

THE SECRET STORIES

The Secret Forest

Hodder
Children's
Books

HODDER CHILDREN'S BOOKS

First published in Great Britain in 1943 by Basil Blackwell
This edition published in 2016 by Hodder and Stoughton

1 3 5 7 9 10 8 6 4 2

Text copyright Hodder and Stoughton
Illustrations copyright Hodder and Stoughton

The moral rights of the author and illustrator have been asserted.

A CIP catalogue record for this book
is available from the British Library.

ISBN 978 1 444 92114 4

Typeset in Caslon Twelve by Avon DataSet Ltd, Bidford on Avon, Warwickshire
Printed in Great Britain by Clays Ltd, St Ives plc

The paper and board used in this book are from well-managed forests
and other responsible sources.

Hodder Children's Books
An imprint of
Hachette Children's Group
Part of Hodder & Stoughton
Carmelite House
50 Victoria Embankment
London EC4Y 0DZ

An Hachette UK Company
www.hachette.co.uk

www.hachettechildrens.co.uk

Contents

1	A Fine Surprise	1
2	Off to Baronia	10
3	The Palace in Baronia	19
4	An Exciting Trip	28
5	Hot Weather!	37
6	Killimooin Castle	46
7	Blind Beowald, the Goatherd	56
8	A Day in the Mountains	67
9	Robbers!	77
10	The Amazing Statue	88
11	The Beginning of the Adventure	99
12	The River in the Mountain	108
13	In the Secret Forest	117
14	Back to the Robber Camp	127
15	A Way of Escape?	135
16	The Terrible Storm	144
17	A Journey up the Mountain River	154
18	In the Cave of the Waterfall	162
19	Beowald to the Rescue!	174
20	The End of the Adventure	183

CHAPTER ONE

A Fine Surprise

THREE EXCITED boys stood on a station platform, waiting for a train to come in.

'The train's late,' said Mike, impatiently. 'Five minutes late already.'

'I'm going to tell the girls the news,' said Jack.

'*I'm* going to tell them!' said Prince Paul, his big dark eyes glowing. 'It's *my* news, not yours.'

'All right, all right,' said Mike. 'You tell Nora and Peggy then, but don't be too long about it or I shall simply have to burst in!'

The three boys were waiting for Nora and Peggy to come back from their boarding school for the summer holidays. Mike, Jack and Prince Paul all went to the same boys' boarding school, and they had broken up the day before. Mike was the twin brother of Nora, and Peggy was his other sister, a year older than Mike and Nora.

Jack was their adopted brother. He had no father or mother of his own, so Captain and Mrs Arnold, the children's father and mother, had taken him into their family, and treated him like another son. He went to boarding school with Mike, and was very happy.

Prince Paul went to the same school too. He was a great friend of theirs, for a year or two back the children had rescued him when he was kidnapped. His father was the King of Baronia, and the little prince spent his term-time at an English boarding school, and his holidays in his own distant land of Baronia. He was the youngest of the five.

'Here comes the train, hurrah!' yelled Mike, as he heard the sound of the train in the distance.

'The girls will be sure to be looking out of the window,' said Jack.

The train came nearer and nearer, and the engine chuffed more and more loudly. It ran alongside the platform, slowed down and stopped. Doors swung open.

Prince Paul gave a yell. 'There they are! Look! In the middle of the train!'

Sure enough, there were the laughing faces of Peggy and Nora, leaning out of the window. Then their door swung open and out leapt the two girls. Nora was dark and curly-haired like Mike. Peggy's golden hair shone in the sun. She had grown taller, but she was still the same old Peggy.

'Peggy! Nora! Welcome back!' yelled Mike. He

hugged his twin sister, and gave Peggy a squeeze too. All five children were delighted to be together again. They had had such adventures, they had shared so many difficulties, dangers and excitements. It was good to be together once more, and say, 'Do you remember this, do you remember that?'

Prince Paul was always a little shy at first when he met the two girls. He held out his hand politely to shake hands, but Peggy gave a squeal and put her arms round him.

'Paul! Don't be such an idiot! Give me a hug!'

'Paul's got some news,' said Mike, suddenly remembering. 'Buck up and tell it, Paul.'

'What is it?' asked Nora.

'I've got an invitation for you all,' said the little prince. 'Will you come to my land of Baronia with me for the holidays?'

There was a shriek of delight from the two girls.

'PAUL! Go to Baronia with you! Oh, I say!'

'Oh! What a marvellous surprise!'

Paul beamed. 'Yes, it is a fine surprise, isn't it?' he said. 'I thought you'd be pleased. Mike and Jack are thrilled too.'

'It will be a real adventure to go to Baronia,' said Mike. 'A country hidden in the heart of mountains – with a few beautiful towns, hundreds of hidden villages, great forests – golly, it will be grand.'

'Oh, Paul, how decent of your father to ask us!' said Nora, putting her arm through the little prince's. 'How long will it take us to get there?'

'We shall fly in my aeroplane,' said Paul. 'Ranni and Pilescu, my two men, will fetch us tomorrow.'

'This is just too good to be true!' said Nora, dancing round in joy. She bumped into a porter wheeling a barrow. 'Oh – sorry, I didn't see you. I say, Mike, we'd better get our luggage. Can you see a porter with an empty barrow?'

All the porters had been engaged, so the five children had to wait. They didn't mind. They didn't mind anything! It was so marvellous to be going off to Paul's country the next day.

'We thought we were going to the seaside with Daddy and Mummy,' said Nora.

'So we were,' said Jack. 'But when Paul's father cabled yesterday, saying he was sending the aeroplane to fetch Paul, he said we were all to come too, if we were allowed to.'

'And you know how Daddy and Mummy like us to travel and see all we can!' said Mike. 'They were just as pleased about it as we were – though they were sorry not to have us for the holidays, of course.'

'We are not to take many clothes,' said Jack. 'Paul says

we can dress up in Baronian things – they are much more exciting than ours! I shall feel I'm wearing fancy dress all the time!'

The girls sighed with delight. They imagined themselves dressed in pretty, swinging skirts and bright bodices – lovely! They would be real Baronians.

'Look here, we really *must* get a porter and stop talking,' said Nora. 'The platform is almost empty. Hi, porter!'

A porter came up, wheeling an empty barrow. He lifted the girls' two trunks on to it and wheeled them down to the barrier. He got a taxi for the children and they all crowded into it. They were to go to their parents' flat for the night.

It was a very happy family party that sat down to a big tea at the flat. Captain and Mrs Arnold smiled round at the five excited faces. To come home for holidays was thrilling enough – but to come home and be told they were all off to Baronia the next day was almost too exciting for words!

Usually the children poured out all the doings of the term – how well they had played tennis, how exciting cricket had been, how fine the new swimming pool was, and how awful the exams were. But today not a word was said about the term that had just passed. No – it was all Baronia, Baronia, Baronia! Paul was delighted to see their excitement, for he was very proud of his country.

'Of course, it is not a very big country,' he said, 'but it is a beautiful one, and a very wild one. Ah, our grand mountains, our great forests, our beautiful villages! The stern rough men, the laughing women, the good food!'

'You sound like a poet, Paul,' said Peggy. 'Go on!'

'No,' said the little prince, going red. 'You will laugh at me. You English people are strange. You love your country but you hardly ever praise her. Now I could tell you of Baronia's beauties for an hour. And not only beauties. I could tell you of wild robbers . . .'

'Oooh,' said Peggy, thrilled.

'And of fierce animals in the mountains,' said Paul.

'We'll hunt them!' Mike chimed in.

'And of hidden ways in the hills, deep forests where no foot has ever trodden, and . . .'

'Oh, let's go this very minute!' said Nora. 'I can't wait! We might have adventures there – thrilling ones, like those we've had before.'

The little prince shook his head. 'No,' he said. 'We shall have no exciting adventures in Baronia. We shall live in my father's palace, and wherever we go there will be guards with us. You see, since that time I was kidnapped, I am never allowed to go about alone in Baronia.'

The other children looked disappointed. 'Well, it

sounds grand to have a bodyguard, I must say, but it does cramp our style a bit,' said Mike. 'Are we allowed to climb trees and things like that?'

'Well, I have never been allowed to in my own country,' said Paul. 'But, you see, I am a prince there, and I have to behave always with much dignity. I behave differently here.'

'I should just think you do!' said Mike, staring at him. 'Who waded through the duck pond to get his ball, and came out covered with mud?'

'And who tore his coat to rags squeezing through a hawthorn hedge, trying to get away from an angry cow?' asked Jack.

'I did,' said Paul. 'But then, here, I am like you. I learn to behave differently. When you go to Baronia you, too, will have different manners. You must kiss my mother's hand, for instance.'

Mike and Jack looked at him in alarm. 'I say! I'm not much good at that sort of thing!' said Jack.

'And you must learn to bow – like this,' said the little prince, thoroughly enjoying himself. He bowed politely from his waist downwards, stood up and brought his heels together with a smart little click. The girls giggled.

'It will be fun to see Mike and Jack doing things like that,' said Nora. 'You'd better start practising now, Mike.

Come on – bow to me. And, Jack, you kiss my hand!'

The boys scowled. 'Don't be an idiot,' said Mike, gruffly. 'If I've got to do it, I will do it – but not to you or Peggy.'

'I don't expect it will be as bad as Paul makes out,' said his mother, smiling. 'He is just pulling your leg. Look at him grinning!'

'You can behave how you like,' said Paul, with a chuckle. 'But don't be surprised at Baronian manners. They are much better than yours!'

'Have you all finished tea?' asked Captain Arnold. 'I can't imagine that any of you could possibly eat any more, but I may be wrong.'

'I'll just have one more piece of cake,' said Mike. 'We don't get chocolate cake like this at school!'

'You've had four pieces already,' said his mother. 'I am glad I don't have to feed you all the year round! There you are – eat it up.'

There was very little packing to be done that evening – only nightclothes and toothbrushes, flannels and things like that. All the children were looking forward to wearing the colourful Baronian clothes. They had seen photographs of the Baronian people, and had very much liked the children's clothes. They were all so thrilled that it was very difficult to settle down and do anything. They talked to Captain and Mrs Arnold, played a game or two and then went off to bed.

Not one of them could go to sleep. They lay in their different bedrooms, calling to one another until Mrs Arnold came up and spoke sternly.

'One more shout – and you don't go to Baronial' After that there was silence, and the five children lay quietly in their beds, thinking of the exciting day tomorrow was going to be.

CHAPTER TWO

Off to Baronia

IT WAS wonderful to wake up the next morning and remember everything. Jack sat up and gave a yell to wake the others. It was not long before everyone was dressed and down to breakfast. They were to go to the airport to meet Ranni and Pilescu, the Baronians, at ten o'clock. All the things they were taking with them went into one small bag.

'Mummy, I'm sorry I won't see much of you these hols,' said Peggy.

'Well, Daddy and I may fly over to Baronia to fetch you back,' said her mother. 'We could come a week or two before it's time for you to return to school, so we should see quite a bit of you!'

'Oh – that would be lovely!' said Nora and Peggy together, and the boys beamed in delight. 'Will you come in the White Swallow?'

The White Swallow was the name given to Captain Arnold's famous aeroplane. In it he and Mrs Arnold had flown many thousands of miles, for they were both excellent pilots. They had had many adventures, and this was partly why they liked their children to go off on their own and have their own adventures too.

'It doesn't do to coddle children too much and shelter them,' said Captain Arnold many a time to his wife. 'We don't want children like that – we want boys and girls of spirit and courage, who can stand on their feet and are not afraid of what may happen to them. We want them to grow up adventurous and strong, of some real use in the world! So we must not say no when a chance comes along to help them to be plucky and independent!'

'If we can grow up like you and Mummy, we shall be all right!' said Peggy. 'You tried to fly all the way to Australia by yourselves in that tiny plane – and you've set up ever so many flying records. We ought to be adventurous children!'

'I think you are,' said her mother, with a laugh. 'You've certainly had some marvellous adventures already – more than most children have all their lives long!'

When the car drew up at the door to take the children to the airport, they all clattered down the steps at once. 'It's a good thing it's a big car!' said Mike. 'Seven of us is quite a crowd!'

Everyone got in. The car set off at a good speed, and

soon came to the big airport. It swept in through the gates. Mike, who was looking out of the window, gave a loud shout.

'There's your aeroplane, Paul! I can see it. It's the smartest one on the airfield.'

'And the loveliest,' said Nora, looking in delight at the beautiful plane towards which they were racing. It was bright blue with silver edges, and it shone brilliantly in the sun. The car stopped a little way from it. Everyone got out. Paul gave a yell.

'There's Pilescu! And Ranni! Look, over there, behind the plane!'

The two big Baronians had heard the engine of the car and they had come to see if it was the children arriving. Pilescu gave a deep-throated shout.

'Paul! My little lord!'

Paul raced over the grass to Pilescu. The big red-bearded man bowed low and then lifted the boy up in his strong arms.

'Pilescu! How are you? It's grand to see you again,' said Paul, in the Baronian language that always sounded so strange to the other children.

Pilescu was devoted to the little prince. He had held him in his arms when he was only a few minutes old, and had vowed to be his man as long as he lived. His arms pressed so tightly round the small boy that Paul gasped for breath.

'Pilescu! I can't breathe! Let me down,' he squealed. Pilescu grinned and set him down. Paul turned to Ranni, who bowed low and then gave him a hug like a bear, almost as tight as Pilescu's.

'Ranni! Have you got any of the chocolate I like so much?' asked Paul. Ranni put his hand into his pocket and brought out a big packet of thick chocolate, wrapped in colourful paper. It had a Baronian name on it. Paul liked it better than any other chocolate, and had often shared it with Mike and Jack, when a parcel had arrived for him from Baronia.

Ranni and Pilescu welcomed the other children, beaming in delight to see them all, and Captain and Mrs Arnold too.

'Look after all these rascals, Pilescu,' said Mrs Arnold, as she said goodbye to the excited children.

'Madam, they are safe with me and with Ranni,' said Pilescu, his red beard flaming in the sun. He bowed from his waist, and took Mrs Arnold's small hand into his big one. He kissed it with much dignity. Mike felt perfectly certain he would never be able to kiss anyone's hand like that.

'Is the plane ready?' asked Captain Arnold, climbing

into the cockpit to have a look round. 'My word, she is a marvellous machine! I'll say this for Baronia – you have some mighty fine designers of aircraft! You beat us hollow, and we are pretty good at it, too.'

All the children were now munching chocolate, talking to Ranni. The big bear-like man was happy to see them.

A mechanic came up and did a few last things to the engine of the great aeroplane. In a minute or two the engines started up and a loud throbbing filled the air.

'Doesn't it sound lovely?' said Mike. 'We're really going!'

'Get in, children,' said Pilescu. 'Say your goodbyes – then we must go.'

The children hugged their parents, and Paul bowed, and kissed Mrs Arnold's hand. She laughed and gave him a squeeze. 'Goodbye, little Paul. Mind you don't lead my four into trouble! Jack, look after everyone. Mike, take care of your sisters. Nora and Peggy, see that the boys don't get up to mischief!'

'Goodbye, Mummy! Goodbye, Daddy! Write to us. Come and fetch us when the hols are nearly over!'

'Goodbye, Captain Arnold! Goodbye, Mrs Arnold!'

The roar of the aeroplane drowned everything. Pilescu was at the controls. Ranni was beside him. The children were sitting behind in comfortable armchairs. The engine roared more loudly.

'R-r-r-r-r-r-r-r! R-r-r-r-r-r-r-r-!' The big machine taxied slowly over the runway – faster – faster – and then, light as a bird, it left the ground, skimmed over the hedges and the trees, and was up in the sky in two minutes.

'Off to Baronia!' said Mike, thrilled.

'Adventuring again,' said Jack. 'Isn't this fun?'

'The runway looks about one inch long!' said Nora, peering out of the window.

'In half an hour we shall be over the sea,' said Paul. 'Let's look out for it.'

It was grand to be in the big aeroplane once more. All the children were used to flying, and loved the feeling of being high up in the sky. Sometimes clouds rolled below them, looking like vast snowfields. The sun shone down on the whiteness, and the clouds below the plane became almost too dazzling to look at.

Suddenly there was a break in the clouds, and Mike gave a yell.

'The sea! Look – through the clouds. Hi, Ranni, Ranni, isn't that the sea already?'

Ranni turned and nodded. 'We are going very fast,' he shouted. 'We want to be in Baronia by lunchtime.'

'I'm so happy,' said Nora, her eyes shining. 'I've always

wanted to go to Baronia, Paul. And now we're really going.'

'I am happy too,' said Paul. 'I like your country, and I like you, too. But I like Baronia better. Maybe you also will like Baronia better.'

'Rubbish!' said Mike. 'As if any country could be nicer than our own!'

'You will see,' said the little prince. 'Have some more chocolate?'

The children helped themselves from Paul's packet. 'Well, I certainly think your chocolate is better than ours,' said Mike, munching contentedly. 'Look, there's the sea again. 'Doesn't it look smooth and flat?'

It was fun watching for the sea to appear and reappear between the gaps in the clouds. Then the plane flew over land again. The clouds cleared away, and the children could see the country below, spread out like an enormous, coloured map.

They flew over great towns, wreathed in misty smoke. They flew over stretches of green countryside, where farms and houses looked like toys. They watched the rivers, curling along like blue and silver snakes. They flew over tall, mountains, and on some of them was snow.

'Funny to see that in the middle of summer,' said Mike. 'How's the time getting on? I say – twelve o'clock already! We shall be there in another hour or so.'

The plane roared along steadily. Ranni took Pilescu's place after two hours had gone by. He sat and talked to the children for a while, gazing devotedly at the little prince. Mike thought he was like a big dog, worshipping his master! He thought Paul was very lucky to have such friends as Ranni and Pilescu.

'Soon we shall see the palace,' he said, looking down. 'Now we are over the borders of Baronia, Paul! Look, there is the river Jollu! And there is the town of Kikibora.'

Paul began to look excited. It was three months since he had been home, and he was longing to see his father and mother, and his little brothers and sisters.

Mike and Jack fell silent. They wondered if Paul's mother would be at the airfield to greet them. Would they have to kiss her hand? 'I shall really feel an awful idiot,' thought Mike, uncomfortably.

'There is the palace!' cried Paul, suddenly. The children saw a palace standing on a hillside – a palace that almost seemed to have come straight from a fairytale! It was a beautiful place, with shining towers and minarets, and below it was a blue lake in which the reflection of the palace shone.

'Oh! It's beautiful!' said Nora. 'Oh, Paul – I feel rather grand. Fancy living in a palace! It may seem ordinary to you – but it's wonderful to me!'

The aeroplane circled round and flew lower. Beside the palace was a great runway, on which the royal planes landed. Ranni's plane swooped low like a bird, its great wheels skimmed the ground, the plane slowed down and came to a halt not far from a little crowd of people.

'Welcome to Baronia!' said Paul, his eyes shining. 'Welcome to Baronia!'

CHAPTER THREE

The Palace in Baronia

RANNI AND Pilescu helped the five children down from the plane. Paul ran straight to a very lovely lady smiling nearby. He bowed low, kissed her hand, and then flung himself on her, chattering quickly in Baronian. It was his mother, the Queen. She laughed and cried at the same time, fondling the little prince's hair, and kissing his cheeks.

Paul's father was there, too, a handsome man, straight and tall, dressed in uniform. Paul saluted him smartly and then leapt into his arms. Then he turned to four smaller children standing nearby, his brothers and sisters. Paul kissed the hands of his little sisters and saluted his brothers. Then they kissed, all talking at once.

Soon it was the other children's turn to say how-do-you-do. They had already met Paul's father and liked him, but they had never seen the little prince's mother. Nora and Peggy thought she looked a real queen, lovely enough to be in a fairy tale. She wore the Baronian dress beautifully, and her full red and blue skirt swung gracefully as she walked.

She kissed Nora and Peggy and spoke to them in English. 'Welcome, little girls!' she said. 'I am so glad to see Paul's friends. You have been so good to him in England. I hope you will be very happy here.'

Then it was the boys' turn to be welcomed. Both of them felt hot and bothered about kissing the Queen's hand, but after all, it was quite easy! Mike stepped forward first, and the Queen held out her hand to him. Mike found himself bending down and kissing it quite naturally! Jack followed, and then they saluted Paul's father.

'Come along to the palace now,' said the Queen. 'You must be very hungry after your long journey. We have all Paul's favourite dishes – and I hope you will like them too.'

The children were glad that Paul's mother could speak English. They had been trying to learn the Baronian language from Paul, but he was not a good teacher. He would go off into peals of laughter at the comical way they pronounced the difficult words of the Baronian language, and it was difficult to get any sense out of him when he was in one of his giggling fits.

The children stared in awe at the palace. They had never seen one like it before, outside of books. It was really magnificent, though not enormous. With the great mountain behind it, and the shining blue lake below, it looked like a dream palace. They walked through a garden full of strange and sweet-smelling flowers and came to a long flight of steps. They climbed these and entered the palace through a wide-open door at which stood six footmen in a line, dressed in the Baronian livery of blue and silver.

After them clattered the little brothers and sisters of Paul, with their nurses. Peggy and Nora thought the small children were sweet. They were all very like Paul, and had big dark eyes.

'We shan't be bothered much with these babies,' said Paul, in rather a lordly voice. 'Of course, they wanted to welcome me. But they live in the nurseries. We shall have our own rooms, and Pilescu will wait on us.'

This was rather a relief to hear. Although the children liked the look of Paul's father and mother very much, they had felt it might be rather embarrassing to live with a king and queen and have meals with them. It was good to hear that they were to be on their own.

Paul took them to their rooms. The girls had a wonderful bedroom overlooking the lake. It was all blue and silver. The ceiling was painted blue with silver stars shining there. The girls thought it was wonderful. The bedspread was the same beautiful blue, embroidered with shining silver stars.

'I shall never dare to sleep in this bed,' said Peggy, in an awed voice. 'It's a four-poster bed – like you see in old pictures – and big enough to take six of us, not two! Oh, Nora – isn't this marvellous fun?'

The boys had two bedrooms between them – one big one for Mike and Jack, with separate beds. 'About half a mile apart!' said Jack, with a laugh, when he saw the enormous bedroom with its two beds, one each end. Paul had a bedroom to himself, leading out of the other one, even bigger!

'However do you manage to put up with living in a dormitory with twelve other boys, when you have a bedroom like this at home?' said Mike to the little prince. 'I say – what a wonderful view!'

Mike's room had two sets of windows. One set looked out over the blue lake and the other looked up the hillside on which the palace was built. It was a grand country.

'It's wild and rugged and rough and beautiful,' said Paul. 'Not like your country. Yours is quite tame. It is like a tame cat, sitting by the fire. Mine is like a wild tiger roaming the hills.'

'He's gone all poetic again!' said Mike, with a laugh. But he knew what Paul meant, all the same. There was something very wild and exciting about Baronia. It looked so beautiful, smiling under the summer sun – but it might not be all it seemed to be on the surface. It was not 'tamed' like their own country – it was still wild, and parts of it quite unknown.

The children washed in basins that seemed to be made of silver. They dried their hands on towels embroidered with the Baronian arms. Everything was perfect. It seemed almost a shame to dirty the towels or make the clear water in the basins dirty and soapy!

They went with Paul to have lunch. They were to have it with the King and Queen, although after that they would have meals in their own playroom, a big room near their bedrooms, which Paul had already shown them. The toys there had made them gasp. An electric railway ran down one side of the room, on which Paul's trains could run. A Meccano set, bigger than any the children had ever seen, was in another corner, with a beautiful bridge made from the pieces, left by Paul from the last holidays. Everything a boy could want was there! It would be great fun to explore that playroom!

The lunch was marvellous. The children did not know any of the dishes, but they all tasted equally delicious. If this was Baronian food they could eat plenty! Paul's mother talked to them in English, and Paul's father made one or two jokes. Paul chattered away to his parents, sometimes in Baronian and sometimes in English. He told them all about the things he did at school.

Jack nudged Mike. 'You'd think Paul was head boy to hear him talk!' he said, in a low tone. 'We'll tease him about this afterwards!'

It was a happy meal. The children were very hungry, but by the time lunch was nearing an end they could not eat another scrap. Jack looked longingly at a kind of pink ice cream with what looked like purple cherries in it. But no – he could not even manage another ice.

Ranni and Pilescu did not eat with the others. They stood quietly, one behind the King's chair and one behind Paul's. A line of soldiers, in the blue and silver uniform, stood at the end of the room. The four English children couldn't help feeling rather grand, eating their lunch with a king, a queen, and a prince, with soldiers on guard at the back. Baronia was going to be fun!

Paul took them all over the palace afterwards. It was a magnificent place, strongly built, with every room flooded with the summer sunshine. The nurseries were full of Paul's younger brothers and sisters. There was a baby in a carved cradle too, covered by a blue and silver rug. It opened big dark eyes when the two girls bent over it.

The nurseries were as lovely as the big playroom that

belonged to Paul. The children stared in wonder at the amount of toys.

'It's like the biggest toyshop I've ever seen!' said Jack. 'And yet, when Paul's at school, the thing he likes best of all is that little old ship I once carved out of a bit of wood!'

Paul was pleased that the others liked his home. He did not boast or show off. It was natural to him to live in a palace and have everything he wanted. He was a warmhearted, friendly little boy who loved to share everything with his friends. Before he had gone to England he had had no friends of his own – but now that he had Mike, Jack, Peggy and Nora, he was very happy. It was marvellous for him to have them with him in Baronia.

'We'll bathe in the lake, and we'll sail to the other side, and we'll go driving in the mountains,' said Paul. 'We'll have a perfectly gorgeous time. I only hope it won't get too hot. If it does, we'll have to go to the mountains where it's cooler.'

The children were very tired by the time that first day came to an end. They seemed to have walked miles in and around the palace, exploring countless rooms, and looking out of countless turrets. They had gone all round the glorious gardens, and had been saluted by numbers of gardeners. Everyone seemed very pleased to see them.

They had tea and supper on the terrace outside the

playroom. Big, colourful umbrellas sheltered the table from the sun. The blue lake shimmered below.

'I wish I hadn't eaten so much lunch,' groaned Mike, as he looked at the exciting array of cakes and biscuits and sandwiches before him. 'I simply don't know what to do. I know I shan't want any supper if I eat this tea – and if supper is anything like lunch, I shall just break my heart if I'm not hungry for it.'

'Oh, you'll be hungry all right,' said Paul. 'Go on – have what you want.'

Before supper the children went for a sail on the lake in Prince Paul's own sailing boat. Ranni went with them. It was lovely and cool on the water. Jack looked at the girls' burnt faces.

'We shall be brown as berries in a day or two,' he said. 'We're all brown now – but we shall get another layer very quickly. My arms are burning! I shan't put them in water tonight! They will sting too much.'

'You'll have to hold your arms above your head when you have your bath, then,' said Mike. 'You will look funny!'

The children were almost too tired to undress and bath themselves that night. Yawning widely they took off their clothes, cleaned their teeth and washed. A bath was sunk into the floor of each bedroom. Steps led down to it. It seemed funny to the children to go down into a bath, instead of just hopping over the side of one. But it was all fun.

The girls got into their big four-poster, giggling. It seemed so big to them after the narrow beds they had at school.

'I shall lose you in the night!' said Nora to Peggy.

The boys jumped into their beds, too. Paul left the door open between his bedroom and that of Mike's and Jack's, so that he might shout to them. But there was very little shouting that night. The children's eyes were heavy and they could not keep them open. The day had been almost too exciting.

'Now we're living in Baronia,' whispered Peggy to herself. 'We're in Baronia, in . . .' And then she was fast asleep, whilst outside the little waves at the edge of the lake lapped quietly all night long.

CHAPTER FOUR

An Exciting Trip

THE FIRST week glided by, golden with sunshine. The children enjoyed themselves thoroughly, though Nora often complained of the heat. All of them now wore the Baronian dress, and fancied themselves very much in it.

The girls wore tight bodices of white and blue, with big silver buttons, and full skirts of red and blue. They wore no stockings, but curious little half-boots, laced up with red. The boys wore embroidered trousers, with cool shirts open at the neck, and a broad belt. They, too, wore the half-boots, and found them very comfortable.

At first they all felt as if they were in fancy dress, but they soon got used to it. 'I shan't like going back to ordinary clothes,' said Nora, looking at herself in the long mirror. 'I do so love the way this skirt swings out round me. Look, Mike – there are yards of material in it.'

Mike was fastening his belt round him. He stuck his scout knife into it. He looked at himself in the mirror, too. 'I look a bit like a pirate or something,' he said. 'Golly, I wish the boys at school could see me now! Wouldn't they be green with envy!'

'They'd laugh at you,' said Nora. 'You wouldn't dare to wear those clothes in England. I hope the Queen will let me take mine back with me. I could wear them at a fancy-dress party. I bet I'd win the prize!'

That first week was glorious. The children were allowed to do anything they wanted to, providing that Ranni or Pilescu was with them. They rode little mountain ponies through the hills. They bathed at least five times a day in the warm waters of the lake. They sailed every evening. They went by car to the nearest big town, and rode in the buses there. They were quaint buses, fat and squat, painted blue and silver. Everything was different, everything was strange.

'England must have seemed very peculiar to you at first, Paul,' said Mike to the little prince, realising for the first time how difficult the boy must have found it living in a strange country.

Paul nodded. He was very happy to show his friends everything. Now, when he was back at school again in England, and wanted to talk about his home and his country, Jack and Mike would understand all he said, and would listen gladly.

Towards the end of the first week Pilescu made a

suggestion. 'Why do you not take your friends in the aeroplane, and show them how big your country is?' he asked Paul. 'I will take you all.'

'Oh yes, Pilescu – let's do that!' cried Mike. 'Let's fly over the mountains and the forests, and see everything!'

'I will show you the Secret Forest,' said Prince Paul, unexpectedly.

The others stared at him. 'What's the Secret Forest?' asked Jack. 'What's secret about it?'

'It's a weird place,' said Paul. 'Nobody has ever been there!'

'Well, how do you know it's there, then?' asked Mike.

'We've seen it from aeroplanes,' said Paul. 'We've flown over it.'

'Why hasn't anyone ever been into this forest?' asked Peggy. 'Someone *must* have, Paul. I don't believe there is anywhere in the whole world that people haven't explored by now.'

'I tell you no one has ever been in the Secret Forest,' said Paul, obstinately. 'And I'll tell you why. Look – get me that map over there, Mike.'

Mike threw him over a rolled-up map. Paul unrolled it and spread it flat on a table. He found the place he wanted and pointed to it.

'This is a map of Baronia,' he said. 'You can see what a

rugged, mountainous country it is. Now look – do you see these mountains here?'

The children bent over to look. The mountains were coloured brown and had an odd name – Killimooin. Paul's brown finger pointed to them. 'These mountains are a weird shape,' said the little prince. 'Killimooin mountains form an almost unbroken circle – and in the midst of them, in a big valley, is the Secret Forest.'

His finger pointed to a tiny speck of green shown in the middle of Killimooin mountains. 'There you are,' he said. 'That dot of green is supposed to be the Secret Forest. It is an enormous forest, really, simply enormous, and goodness knows what wild animals there are there.'

'Yes, but Paul, *why* hasn't anyone been to see?' asked Mike, impatiently. 'Why can't they just climb the mountains and go down the other side to explore the forest?'

'For a very good reason!' said Paul. 'No one has ever found a way over Killimooin mountains!'

'Why? Are they so steep?' asked Nora, astonished.

'Terribly steep, and terribly dangerous,' said Paul.

'Does anyone live on the mountainsides?' asked Peggy.

'Only goatherds,' said Paul. 'But they don't climb very high because the mountains are so rocky and so steep. Maybe the goats get to the top – but the goatherds don't!'

'Well!' said Mike, fascinated by the idea of a secret forest that no one had ever explored. 'This really is exciting, I must say. Do, do let's fly over it in your aeroplane, Paul. Wouldn't I just love to see what that forest is like!'

'You can't see much,' said Paul, rolling up the map. 'It just looks a thick mass of green that's all, from the plane. All right – we'll go tomorrow!'

This was thrilling. It would be grand to go flying again, and really exciting to roar over the Killimooin mountains and peer down at the Secret Forest. What animals lived there? What would it be like there? Had anyone ever trodden its dim green paths? Mike and Jack wished a hundred times they could explore that great hidden forest!

The next day all five children went to the runway beside the hangar where Paul's aeroplane was kept. They watched the mechanics run it out on to the grass. They greeted Ranni and Pilescu as the two men came along.

'Ranni! Do you know the way to fly to Killimooin mountains? We want to go there!'

'And when we get there, fly as low down as you can, so that we can get as near to the Secret Forest as possible,' begged Nora.

Ranni and Pilescu smiled. They climbed up into the

aeroplane. 'We will go all round Baronia,' said Pilescu, 'and you will see, we shall fly over Killimooin country. It is wild, very wild. Not far from it is the little palace the King built last year, on a mountainside where the winds blow cool. The summers have been very hot of late in Baronia, and it is not healthy for children. Maybe you will all go there if the sun becomes much hotter!'

'I hope we do!' said Paul, his eyes shinning. 'I've never been there, Pilescu. We should have fun there, shouldn't we?'

'Not the same kind of fun as you have in the big palace,' said Pilescu. 'It is wild and rough around the little palace. It is more like a small castle. There are no proper roads. You can have no car, no aeroplane. Mountain ponies are all you would have to get about on.'

'I'd like that,' said Jack. He took his seat in the big plane, and watched the mechanics finishing their final checks on the plane. They moved out of the way. The engine started up with a roar. Nobody could hear a word.

Then off went the big plane, as smoothly as a car, taxiing over the grass. The children hardly knew when it rose in the air. But when they looked from the windows, they saw the earth far below them. The palace seemed no bigger than a doll's house.

'We're off!' said Jack, with a sigh. 'Where is the map?

You said you'd bring one, Paul, so that we could see exactly where we are each minute.'

It really was interesting to spread out the "map, and try to find exactly where they were. 'Here we are!' said Jack, pointing to a blue lake on the map. 'See? There's the lake down below us now – we're right over it – and look, there's the river flowing into it, shown on the map. Golly, this is geography really come alive! I wish we could learn this sort of geography at school! I wouldn't mind having geography every morning of the week, if we could fly over the places we're learning about!'

The children read out the names of the towns they flew over. 'Ortanu, Tarribon, Lookinon, Brutinlin – what funny names!'

'Look – there are mountains marked here. We ought to reach them soon.'

'The plane is going up. We must be going over them. Yes – we are. Look down and see. Golly, that's a big one over there!'

'Aren't the valleys green? And look at that river. It's like a silvery snake.'

'Are we coming near the Secret Forest? Are we near Killimooin? Blow, I've lost it again on the map. I had it a minute ago.'

'Your hand's over it, silly! Move it, Jack – yes, there,

look! Killimooin. We're coming to the mountains!'

Ranni yelled back to the children. 'Look out for the Secret Forest! We are coming to the Killimooin range now. Paul, you know it. Look out now, and tell the others.'

In the greatest excitement the five children pressed their faces against the windows of the big plane. It was rising over steep mountains. The children could see how wild and rugged they were. They could not see anyone on them at all, nor could they even see a house.

'Now you can see how the Killimooin mountains run all round in a circle!' cried Paul. 'See – they make a rough ring, with their rugged heads jagged against the sky! There is no valley between, no pass! No one can get over them into the Secret Forest that lies in the middle of their mighty ring!'

The children could easily see how the range of mountains ran round in a very rough circle. Shoulder to shoulder stood the rearing mountains, tall, steep and wild.

The aeroplane roared over the edge of the circle, and the children gazed down into the valley below.

'That's the Secret Forest!' shouted Paul. 'See, there it is. Isn't it thick and dark? It fills the valley almost from end to end.'

The Secret Forest lay below the roaring, throbbing plane. It was enormous. The tops of the great trees stood close together, and not a gap could be seen. The plane roared low down over the trees.

'It's mysterious!' said Nora, and she shivered. 'It's really mysterious. It looks so quiet – and dark – and lonely. Just as if really and truly nobody ever has set foot there, and never will!'

CHAPTER FIVE

Hot Weather!

THE AEROPLANE rose high again to clear the other side of the mountain ring. The forest dwindled smaller and smaller. 'Go back again over the forest, Ranni, please do!' begged Jack. 'It's weird. So thick and silent and gloomy. It gives me a funny feeling!'

Ranni obligingly swung the big plane round and swooped down over the forest again. The trees seemed to rise up, and it almost looked as if the aeroplane was going to dive down into the thick green!

'Wouldn't it be awful if our plane came down in the forest, and we were lost there, and could never, never find our way out and over the Killimooin mountains?' said Nora.

'What a horrid thought!' said Peggy. 'Don't say things like that! Ranni, let's get over the mountains quickly! I'm afraid we might get lost here!'

Ranni laughed. He swooped upwards again, just as Jack spotted something that made him flatten his nose against the window and stare hard.

'What is it?' asked Nora.

'I don't quite know,' said Jack. 'It couldn't be what I thought it was, of course.'

'What did you think it was?' asked Paul, as they flew high over the other side of the mountain ring.

'I thought it was a spiral of smoke,' said Jack. 'It couldn't have been, of course – because where there is smoke, there is a fire, and where there is a fire, there are men! And there are no men down there in the Secret Forest!'

'*I* didn't see any smoke,' said Mike.

'Nor did I,' said Paul. 'It must have been a wisp of low-lying cloud, Jack.'

'Yes – it must have been,' said Jack. 'But it *did* look like smoke. You know how sometimes on a still day the smoke from a camp fire rises almost straight into the air and stays there for ages. Well, it was like that.'

'I think the Secret Forest is very, very strange and mysterious,' said Peggy. 'And I never want to go there!'

'I would, if I got the chance!' said Mike. 'Think of walking where nobody else had ever put their foot! I would feel a real explorer.'

'This is Jonnalongay,' called Ranni from the front. 'It is one of our biggest towns, set all round a beautiful lake.'

The children began to take an interest in the map again. It was such fun to see a place on the big map, and then to watch it coming into view below, as the aeroplane flew towards it. But soon after that they flew into thick cloud and could see nothing.

'Never mind,' said Ranni. 'We have turned back now, and are flying along the other border of Baronia. It is not so interesting here. The clouds will probably clear just about Tirriwutu, and you will see the railway lines there. Watch out for them.'

Sure enough, the clouds cleared about Tirriwutu, and the children saw the gleaming silver lines, as Pilescu took the great plane down low over the flat countryside. It was fun to watch the lines spreading out here and there, going to different little villages, then joining all together again as they went towards the big towns.

'Oh – there's the big palace by the lake!' said Nora, half-disappointed. 'We're home again. That was simply lovely, Paul.'

'But the nicest part was Killimooin and the Secret Forest,' said Jack. 'I don't know why, but I just can't get that mysterious forest out of my head. Just suppose that *was* smoke I saw! It would mean that people live there – people no one knows about – people who can't get out and never could! What are they like, I wonder?'

'Don't be silly, Jack,' said Mike. 'It wasn't smoke, so there aren't people. Anyway, if people are living there now, they must have got over the mountains at some time or other, mustn't they? So they could get out again if they wanted to! Your smoke was just a bit of cloud. You know what funny bits of cloud we see when we're flying.'

'Yes, I know,' said Jack. 'You're quite right, it couldn't have been real smoke. But I rather like to think it was, just for fun. It makes it all the more mysterious!'

The aeroplane flew down to the runway, and came to a stop. The mechanics came running up.

'You have had the best of it today!' one called to Ranni, in the Baronian language, which the children were now beginning to understand. 'We have almost melted in the heat! This sun – it is like a blazing furnace!'

The heat from the parched ground came to meet the children as they stepped out of the plane. Everything shimmered and shook in the hot sun.

'Gracious!' said Nora. 'I shall melt! Oh for an ice cream!'

They walked to the palace and lay down on sunbeds on the terrace, under the big colourful umbrellas. Usually there was a little wind from the lake on the terrace – but today there was not a breath of air.

'Shall we bathe?' said Jack.

'No good,' said Mike. 'The water was too warm to be

pleasant yesterday – and I bet it's really hot today. It gets like a hot bath after a day like this.'

A big gong boomed through the palace. It was time for lunch – a late one for the children. Nora groaned.

'It's too hot to eat! I can't move. I don't believe I could even swallow an ice cream!'

'Lunch is indoors for you today,' announced Ranni, coming out on to the terrace. 'It is cooler indoors. The electric fans are all going in the playroom. Come and eat.'

None of the children could eat very much, although the dishes were just as delicious as ever. Ranni and Pilescu, who always served the children at mealtimes, looked quite worried.

You must eat, little prince,' Ranni said to Paul.

'It's too hot,' said Paul. 'Where's my mother? I'm going to ask her if I need wear any clothes except shorts. That's all they wear in England in the summer, when it's holiday time and hot.'

'But you are a prince!' said Ranni. 'You cannot run about with hardly anything on.'

Prince Paul went to find his mother. She was lying down in her beautiful bedroom, a scented handkerchief lying over her eyes.

'Mother! Are you ill?' asked Paul.

'No, little Paul – only tired with this heat,' said his

mother. 'But listen, we will go to the mountains to the little castle your father built there last year. I fear that this heat will kill us all! Your father says he will send us tomorrow. How we shall get there with all the children and the nurses I cannot imagine! But go we must! I don't know what has happened these last few years in Baronia! The winters are so cold and the summers are so hot!'

Paul forgot that he had come to ask if he could take off his clothes. He stared at his mother, thrilled and excited. To go to the mountains to the new little castle! That would be fine. The children could explore the country on mountain ponies. They would have a great time. The winds blew cool on the mountainside, and they would not feel as if they wanted to lie about and do nothing all day long. 'Oh, mother! Shall we really go tomorrow?' said Paul. 'I'll go and tell the others.'

He sped off, forgetting how hot he was. He burst into the playroom, and the others looked at him in amazement.

'However can you possibly race about like that in this heat?' asked Jack. 'You must be mad! I'm dripping wet just lying here and doing nothing.'

'We're going to the new little castle in the mountains tomorrow!' cried Paul. There's news for you! It will be cool there, and we can each have a pony and go riding up and down the mountains. We can talk to the goatherds, and have all kinds of fun!'

Jack sat up. 'I say!' he said. 'Did you hear Pilescu say that your new little palace was near Killimooin? Golly, what fun! We might be able to find out something about the Secret Forest!'

'We shan't!' said Paul. 'There's nothing to find out. You can ask the goatherds there and see. Won't it be fun to go and stay in the wild mountains? I *am* glad!'

All the children were pleased. It really was too hot to enjoy anything in the big palace now. The idea of scampering about the mountains on sturdy little ponies was very delightful. Jack lay back on the couch and wondered if it would be possible to find out anything about the Secret Forest. He would ask every goatherd he saw whether he could tell anything about that mysterious forest, hidden deep in the heart of Killimooin.

'If anyone knows anything, the goatherds should know,' thought the boy. Then he spoke aloud. 'Paul, how do we go to the mountains where the little castle is? Do we ride on ponies?'

'No – we drive most of the way,' said Paul. 'But as there is no proper road within twenty miles, we shall have to go on ponies for the rest of the way. I don't know how the younger children will manage.'

'This is a lovely holiday!' said Nora, dreamily. 'Living in a palace – flying about in aeroplanes – peering down at the Secret Forest – and now going to live in a castle built in the wild mountains, where there is not even a proper road. We *are* lucky!'

'It's getting hotter,' said Mike, with a groan. 'Even the draught from the electric fan seems hot! I hope it will get a bit cooler by the time the evening comes.'

But it didn't. It seemed to get hotter than ever. Not one of the five children could sleep, though the fans in their big bedrooms went all night long. They flung off the sheets. They turned their pillows to find a cool place. They got out of bed and stood by the open windows to find a breath of air.

By the time the morning came they were a heavy-eyed, cross batch of children, ready to quarrel and squabble over anything. Paul flew into a temper with Ranni, and the big man laughed.

'Ah, my little lord, this heat is bad for you all! Now do not lose your temper with me. That is foolish, for if you become hot-tempered, you will feel hotter than ever! Go and get ready. The cars will be here in half an hour.'

The boys went to have cool baths. It was too hot to swim in the lake, which was just like a warm bath now. They came out of the cold water feeling better. Mike heard the noise of car engines, and went to the window. A perfect fleet of cars was outside, ready to take the whole family, with the exception of Paul's father. The five older children, the five young ones, Paul's mother, three nurses, and Ranni and Pilescu were all going.

'Come on!' yelled Paul. 'We're going. Nora, you'll be left behind. Hurry up!'

And into the cars climbed all the royal household, delighted to be going into the cool mountains at last.

CHAPTER SIX

Killimooin Castle

IT TOOK quite a time to pack in all the five younger children. One of the nurses had the baby in a big basket beside her. The other nursery children chattered and laughed. They looked pale with the heat, but they were happy at the thought of going to a new place.

Ranni and Pilescu travelled with the four English children and Prince Paul. There was plenty of room in the enormous blue and silver car. Nora was glad when at last they all set off, and a cool draught came in at the open windows. The little girl felt ill with the blazing summer heat of Baronia.

'The new castle is called Killimooin Castle,' announced Paul. 'I've never seen it myself, because it was built when I was away. It's actually on one of the slopes of Killimooin. We can do a bit of exploring.'

'You will not go by yourselves,' said Ranni. 'There may be robbers and wild men there.'

'Oh, Ranni – we must go off by ourselves sometimes!'

cried Jack. 'We can't have you always hanging round us like a nursemaid.'

'You will not go by yourselves,' repeated Ranni, a little sternly, and Pilescu nodded in agreement.

'Killimooin is about two hundred miles away,' said Paul. 'We ought to get there in four or five hours – as near there as the roads go, anyway.'

The great cars purred steadily along at a good speed. There were five of them, for servants had been taken as well. Behind followed a small van with a powerful engine. In the van were all the things necessary for the family in the way of clothes, prams and so on.

The countryside flew by. The children leaned out of the windows to get the air. Ranni produced some of the famous Baronian chocolate, that tasted as much of honey and cream as of chocolate. The children munched it and watched the rivers, hills and valleys they passed. Sometimes the road wound around a mountainside, and Nora turned her head away so that she would not see down into the valley, so many hundreds of feet below. She said it made her feel giddy.

'I don't know what we would do if we met another car on these curving roads that wind up and up the mountainside,' said Peggy.

'Oh, the roads have been cleared for us,' said Paul. 'We shan't meet any cars on the mountain roads, anyway, so you needn't worry.'

They didn't. The cars roared along, stopping for nothing – nothing except lunch! At half-past twelve, when everyone was feeling very hungry, the signal was given to stop. They all got out to stretch their legs and have a run round. They were on a hillside, and below them ran a shining river, curving down the valley. It was a lovely place for a picnic.

As usual the food was delicious. Ranni and Pilescu unpacked hampers and the children spread a snow-white cloth on the grass and set out plates and dishes.

'Chicken sandwiches! Good!' said Mike.

'Ice cream pudding! My favourite!' said Nora.

'About thirty different kinds of sandwiches!' said Jack. 'I am glad I feel so terribly hungry.'

It was a good meal, sitting out there on the hillside, where a little breeze blew.

'It's cooler already,' said Nora, thankfully.

'It will be much cooler in Killimooin Castle,' said Ranni. 'It is built in a cunning place, where two winds meet round a gully! It is always cool there on the hottest day. You will soon get back your rosy cheeks.'

Everyone climbed back into the cars when lunch was

finished, and off they went again. 'Only about an hour more and the road ends for us,' said Pilescu, looking at his watch. 'It goes on round the mountains, but leaves Killimooin behind. I hope the ponies will be there, ready for us.'

'How is the baby going to ride a pony?' asked Nora. 'Won't she fall off?'

'Oh, no,' said Pilescu. 'You will see what happens to the little ones.'

After about an hour, all the cars slowed down and stopped. The children looked out in excitement, for there was quite a gathering in front of them. Men with ponies stood there, saluting the cars. It was time to mount and ride, instead of sitting in a car!

It took a long time to get everyone on to the sturdy, shaggy little ponies. Nora soon saw how the little children were taken! The bigger ponies had a big, comfortable basket strapped each side of them – and into these the younger children were put! Then with a man leading each pony, the small ones were quite safe, and could not possibly fall!

'I'm not going in a basket,' said Nora, half afraid she might be told to. But all the other children could ride and were expected to do so. Each child sprang on to the pony brought beside him or her and held the reins. The ponies were stout and steady, very easy to ride, though Nora complained that hers bumped her.

'Ah no, Nora – it is you who are bumping the pony!' said Pilescu, with a laugh.

The little company set off. The nurses, who had all been country girls, thought nothing of taking their children on ponies to the castle. The smaller boys and girls chattered in high voices and laughed in delight at the excitement.

The men leading the ponies that carried baskets or panniers leapt on to ponies also, and all the little sturdy animals trotted away up the rough mountain path that led to the new castle. The people who had come to watch the royal family's arrival waved goodbye and shouted good wishes after them. Their cottages were here and there in the distance.

The little company turned a bend in the path, and then the children saw the towering mountains very clearly, steep and forbidding, but very grand. Up and up they had to go, climbing higher little by little towards the castle Paul's father had built the year before. No houses, no cottages were to be seen. It was very desolate indeed.

'Look at those goats!' said Peggy, pointing to a flock of goats leaping up the rocky slopes. 'What a lot of them! Where's the goatherd?'

'Up there,' said Paul. 'Look – by that crooked tree.'

The goatherd stared down at the company. He had the flaming red beard that most Baronians had, and he wore ragged trousers of goat-skin, and nothing else.

'He looks awfully wild and fierce,' said Nora. 'I don't think I want to talk to goatherds if they look like that!'

'Oh, they are quite harmless!' said Ranni, laughing at Nora's scared face. 'They would be more frightened of you than you would be of them!'

It was fun at first to jog along on the ponies for the first few miles, but when the road grew steeper, and wound round and round, the children began to wish the long journey was over.

'There's one thing, it's lovely and cool,' said Jack.

'It will be quite cold at nights,' said Ranni. 'You will have to sleep with thick covers over you.'

'Well, that will be a change,' said Jack, thinking of how he had thrown off everything the night before and had yet been far too hot. 'I say – I say – is that Killimooin Castle?'

It was. It stood up there on the mountainside, overlooking a steep gully, built of stones quarried from the mountain itself. It did not look new, and it did not look old. It looked exactly right, Nora thought. It was small, with rounded towers, and roughly hewn steps, cut out of the mountain rock, led up to it.

'I shall feel as if I'm living two or three hundred years

ago, when I'm in that castle,' said Peggy. 'It's a proper little castle, not an old ruin, or a new make-believe one. I do like it. Killimooin Castle – it just suits it, doesn't it?'

'Exactly,' said Jack. 'It's about halfway up the mountain, isn't it? We're pretty high already.'

So they were. Although the mountains still towered above them, the valley below looked a very long way down. The wind blew again and Nora shivered.

'Golly, I believe I shall be too cold now!' she said, with a laugh.

'Oh, no – it's only the sudden change from tremendous heat to the coolness of the mountains that you feel,' said Ranni. 'Are you tired? You will want a good rest before tea!'

'Oh, isn't it nearly teatime?' said Mike, in disappointment. 'I feel so hungry. Look – we're nearly at that fine flight of steps. I'm going to get off my pony.'

The caretakers of the castle had been looking out for the royal arrivals. They stood at the top of the flight of steps, the big, iron-studded door open behind them. The children liked them at once.

'That is Tooku, with Yamen his wife,' said Pilescu. 'They are people from the mountains here. You will like to talk to them sometime, for they know many legends and stories of these old hills.'

Tooku and Yamen greeted the children with cries of delight and joy. They were cheerful mountain-folk, not scared at the thought of princes and princesses arriving, but full of joy to see so many little children.

It seemed no time at all before the whole company were in their new quarters. These were not nearly so grand and luxurious as those the children had had in the big palace, but not one of them cared about that. The castle rooms were small, but with high ceilings. The walls were hung with old embroidered tapestries. There were no curtains at the narrow windows – but, oh, the view from those windows!

Mountains upon mountains could be seen, some wreathed in clouds, most of them with snow on the top. The trees on them looked like grass. The valley below seemed miles away.

'Killimooin Castle has quite a different feel about it,' said Jack, with enjoyment. 'The palace was big and modern and everything was up to date. Killimooin is grim and strong and wild, and I like it. There's no hot water running in the bedrooms. I haven't seen a bathroom yet – and our beds are more like rough couches with rugs and pillows than beds. I do like it.'

It was great fun settling down in the castle. The children could go anywhere they liked, into the kitchens, the towers, the cellars. Tooku and Yamen welcomed them anywhere and anytime.

It was deliciously cool at Killimooin after the tremendous heat of the palace. The children slept well that first night, enjoying the coolness of the air that blew in at the narrow windows. It was good mountain air, clean and scented with pine.

Next morning Ranni spoke to the five children. 'You have each a pony to ride, and you may ride when and where you will, if Pilescu or I are with you.'

'Why can't we go alone?' said Paul, rather sulkily. 'We shan't come to any harm.'

'You might lose your way in the mountains,' said Ranni. 'It is an easy thing to do. You must promise never to wander off without one of us.'

Nobody wanted to promise. It wasn't nearly so much fun to go about with a grown-up, as by themselves. But Ranni was firm.

'You must promise,' he repeated. 'No promise, no ponies. That is certain!'

'I suppose we must promise, then,' said Jack. 'All right – I promise not to go wandering off without a nursemaid!'

'I promise too,' said Mike. The girls promised as well.

'And you, little lord?' said big Ranni, turning to the still-sulky boy.

'Well – I promise too,' said Paul. 'But there isn't any real danger, I'm sure!'

Paul was wrong. There *was* danger – but not the kind that anyone guessed.

CHAPTER SEVEN

Blind Beowald, the Goatherd

TWO DAYS later a great mist came over Killimooin and not even Ranni and Pilescu dared to ride out on their ponies, although they had said that they would take the children exploring round about.

'No one can see his way in such a mist,' said Ranni, looking out of the window. 'The clouds lie heavy over the valley below us. Up here the mist is so thick that we might easily leave the mountain path and go crashing down the mountain-side.'

'It's so disappointing,' sighed Paul. 'What can we do instead?'

Yamen put her head in at the door as she passed. 'You can come down to tea with Tooku and me,' she invited. 'We will have something nice for you, and you shall ask us all the things you want to know.'

'Oh, good,' said Jack. 'We'll ask all about the Secret Forest. Maybe they know tales about that! That will be exciting.'

Teatime down in the big kitchen of the castle was great

fun. An enormous fire glowed on the big hearth, and over it hung a black pot in which the soup for the evening meal was slowly simmering. A grand tea was spread on the wooden table, and the children enjoyed it. There were no thin sandwiches, no dainty buns and biscuits, no cream cakes – but, instead, there were hunks of new-made bread, baked by Yamen that morning, crisp rusks with golden butter, honey from the wild bees, and an unusual, rich cake with a bittersweet taste that was delicious.

'Yamen, tell us all you know about the Secret Forest,' begged Nora, as she buttered a rusk. 'We have seen it when we flew over in an aeroplane. It was so big and so mysterious.'

'The Secret Forest!' said Yamen. 'Ah, no one knows anything of that. It is lost in the mountains, a hidden place unknown to man.'

'Doesn't anyone live there at all?' asked Jack, remembering the spire of smoke he thought he had seen.

'How could they?' asked Tooku, in his deep, hoarse voice, from the end of the table. 'There is no way over Killimooin mountains.'

'Hasn't anyone *ever* found a way?' asked Jack.

Tooku shook his head. 'No. There is no way. I have heard it said, however, that there is a steep way to the top, whence one can see this great forest – but there is no way down the other side – no, not even for a goat!'

The children listened in silence. It was disappointing to hear that there really was no way at all. Tooku ought to know, for he had lived among the mountains for years.

'Ranni won't let us go about alone,' complained Paul. 'It makes us feel so babyish, Tooku. Can't you tell him the mountains are safe?'

'They are not safe,' said Tooku, slowly. 'There are robbers. I have seen them from this very castle. Ah, when this place was built last year, the robbers must have hoped for travellers to come to and fro!'

'What robbers?' asked Jack. 'Where do they live? Are there many of them?'

'Yes, there are many,' said Tooku, nodding his shaggy head. 'Sometimes they rob the poor people of the countryside, coming in the night, and taking their goats and their hens. Sometimes they rob the travellers on the far-off road.'

'Why aren't they caught and punished?' demanded the little prince indignantly. 'I won't have robbers in my country!'

'No one knows where these robbers live,' said Yamen. 'Aie-aie – they are a terrible band of men. It is my belief that they have a stronghold far up the mountains.'

'Perhaps they live in the Secret Forest!' said Jack.

'Oh, you and your Secret Forest!' said Nora. 'Don't keep asking about it, Jack. You've been told ever so many times there's no way for people to get to it.'

'Are there any wild animals about the mountains?' asked Mike.

'There are wolves,' said Yamen. 'We hear them howling in the cold wintertime, when they can find no food. Yes, they came even to this castle, for I saw them myself.'

'How frightening!' said Nora, shivering. 'Well, I'm jolly glad I promised Ranni I wouldn't go out without him or Pilescu! I don't want to be captured by robbers or caught by wolves.'

'You don't want to believe all their stories,' said Peggy, in a low voice.

Yamen heard her, and although she did not understand what the little girl said, she guessed.

'Ah!' she said, 'you think these are but tales, little one? If you want to know more, go to the goatherd, Beowald, and he will tell you many more strange tales of the mountainside!'

Beowald sounded rather exciting, the children thought. They asked where he could be found.

'Take the path that winds high above the castle,' said Tooku. 'When you come to a crooked pine, struck by lightning, take the goat-track that forks to the left. It is a rocky way, but your ponies will manage it well. Follow this track until you come to a spring gushing out beside a big rock. Shout for Beowald, and he will hear you, for his ears are like that of a mountain hare, and he can hear the growing of the grass in spring, and the flash of a shooting star in November!'

The next day was fine and clear. The children reminded Ranni of his promise and he grinned at them, his eyes shining in the brilliant sunlight.

'Yes, we will go,' he said. 'I will get the ponies. We will take our lunch with us and explore.'

'We want to find Beowald the goatherd,' said Paul. 'Have you heard of him, Ranni?'

Ranni shook his head. He went to get the ponies, whilst Nora and Peggy ran off to ask Yamen to pack them up some lunch.

Soon they were all ready. Ranni made them take thick Baronian cloaks, lined with fur, for he said that if a mist suddenly came down they would feel very cold indeed.

They set off up the steep mountain-way that wound high above the castle. The ponies were sure-footed on the rocky path, though they sent hundreds of little pebbles clattering down the mountainside as they went. They were nice little beasts, friendly and eager, and the children were already very fond of them.

Ranni led the way, Pilescu rode last of all. It was a merry little company that went up the steep mountain that sunny morning.

'We've got to look out for a crooked pine tree, struck by lightning,' said Jack to Ranni, who was just in front of him. Then we take the goat-track to the left.'

'There's an eagle!' said Nora, suddenly, as she saw a great bird rising into the air, its wings spreading out against the sun. 'Are eagles dangerous, Pilescu?'

'They will not attack us,' said Ranni. 'They like to swoop down on the little kids that belong to the goats and take them to feed their young ones, if they are nesting.'

'I wonder if we shall see a wolf,' said Peggy, hoping that they wouldn't. 'I say, isn't it fun riding up and up like this! I do like it.'

'There's the crooked pine tree!' shouted Paul. 'Look – over there. We shall soon come up to it. Isn't it ugly? You don't often see a pine tree that is not tall and straight.'

The crooked pine tree seemed to point to the left, where the path forked into two. To the left was a narrow goat-track, and the ponies took that way, their steady little hooves clattering along merrily.

It was lovely up there in the cool clear air, with the valley far below, swimming in summer sunshine. Sometimes a little wispy cloud floated below the children, and once one floated right into them. But it was nothing but a mist when the children found themselves in it!

'Clouds are only mists,' said Nora. 'They look so solid when you see them sailing across the sky, especially those mountainous, piled-up clouds that race across in March and April – but they're nothing but mist!'

'What's that noise?' said Jack, his sharp ears hearing something.

'Water bubbling somewhere,' said Nora, stopping her pony. 'It must be the spring gushing out, that Tooku and Yamen told us about. We must be getting near where Beowald should be.'

'Look at the goats all about,' said Peggy, and she pointed up the mountainside. There were scores of goats there, some staring at the children in surprise, some leaping from rock to rock in a hair-raising manner.

'Goats have plenty of circus tricks,' said Mike, laughing as he watched a goat take a flying leap from a rocky ledge, and land with all four feet bunched together on a small rock not more than six inches square. 'Off he goes again! I wonder they don't break their legs.'

'They must be Beowald's goats,' said Peggy. 'Ranni, call Beowald.'

But before Ranni could shout, another noise came to the children's ears. It was a strange, plaintive noise, like a peculiar melody with neither beginning nor end. It was odd, and the children listened, feeling a little uncomfortable.

'Whatever's that?' asked Peggy.

They rode on a little way and came to a big rock beside which gushed a clear spring, running from a rocky hole in the mountainside. On the other side, in the shelter of the rock, lay a youth, dressed only in rough trousers of goat-skin. Round his neck, tied by a leather cord, was a kind of flute, and on this the goatherd was playing his strange, unending melodies.

He sat up when the children dismounted. The children saw that his strange dark eyes were blind. There was no light in them. They could see nothing. But it was a happy face they looked on, and the goatherd spoke to them in a deep, musical voice.

'You are come!' he said. 'I heard you down the mountain two hours since. I have been waiting for you.'

'How did you know we were coming to see you?' asked Paul in astonishment.

Beowald smiled. It was a strange smile, for although his mouth curved upwards, his eyes remained empty and dark.

'I knew,' said Beowald. 'I know all that goes on in my mountains. I know the eagles that soar above my head. I know the wolves that howl in the night. I know the small flowers that grow beneath my feet, and the big trees that give me shade. I know Killimooin as no one else does.'

'Well, Beowald, do you know anything about the Secret Forest then?' asked Paul, eagerly. The other children could now understand what was said in the Baronian language, though they were not able to speak it very well as yet. They listened eagerly for Beowald's answer.

Beowald shook his head. 'I could take you where you can see it,' he said. 'But there is no way to it. My feet have followed my goats everywhere in these mountains, even to the summits – but never have they leapt down the other side. Not even for goats is there any path.'

The children were disappointed. 'Are there robbers here?' asked Jack, trying to speak in Baronian. Beowald understood him.

'Sometimes I hear strange men at night,' he said. 'They creep down the mountain path, and they call to one another as the owls do. Then I am afraid and I hide in my cave, for these robbers are fierce and wild. They are like the wolves that roam in the winter, and they seek men to rob and slay.'

'Where do the robbers live?' asked Paul, puzzled.

Beowald shook his head, gazing at the little prince with his dark blind eyes. 'That is a thing I have never known,' he said. 'They are men without a home. Men without a dwelling-place. That is why I fear them. They cannot be human, these men, for all men have a dwelling-place.'

'That's silly,' said Jack, in English. 'All men have to live somewhere, even robbers! Paul, ask Beowald if they could live somewhere in a mountain cave, as he does.'

Paul asked the goatherd, but he shook his head. 'I know every cave in the mountains,' he said. 'They are my caves, for only I set foot in them. I live up here all the summer, and only in the cold winter do I go down to the valley to be with my mother. In the good weather I am happy here, with my goats and my music.'

'Play to us again,' begged Peggy. The goatherd put his wooden flute to his lips and began to play a strange little tune. The goats around lifted their heads and listened. The little kids came quite near. A great old goat, with enormous curling horns, stepped proudly up to Beowald and put his face close to the goatherd's.

Beowald changed the tune. Now it was no longer like the spring that ran down the mountainside, bubbling to itself. It was like the gusty wind that blew down the hills and swept up the valleys, that danced and capered and shouted over the pine trees and the graceful birches.

The children wanted to dance and caper too. The goats felt the change in the music and began to leap about madly. It was an odd sight to see. Jack looked at the blind youth's face. It was completely happy. Goats, mountains – and music. Beowald wanted nothing more in his quiet, lonely life!

CHAPTER EIGHT

A Day in the Mountains

'CAN'T WE have lunch here with Beowald?' asked Paul, suddenly. 'I feel very hungry, Ranni. It would be lovely to sit here in the wind and the sun and eat our food, listening to Beowald.'

'I expect the goatherd would rather eat with you than play whilst you gobble up all the food!' said Ranni with a laugh. 'Ask him if he will eat with you.'

The goatherd smiled when he heard what Ranni said. He nodded his head, gave an order that scattered his goats, and sat quite still, gazing out over the valleys below as if he could see everything there.

'Where do you sleep at night?' asked Paul. 'Where is your cave?'

'Not far from here,' answered Beowald. 'But often I sleep in the daytime and walk at night.'

'But how can you find your way then?' said Peggy, thinking of the darkness of the mountainside and its dangerous ledges and precipices.

'It is always dark for me,' said Beowald. 'My ears see

for me, and my feet see for me. I can wander in these mountains for hours and yet know exactly where I am. The pebbles beneath my feet, the rocks, the grass, the flowers, they all tell me where I am. The smell of the pine trees, the scent of the wild thyme that grows nearby, the feel of the wind, they tell me too. I can go more safely over this steep mountain with my blind eyes than you could go, seeing all there is to be seen!'

The children listened to the blind goatherd, as Ranni and Pilescu set out the lunch. There were sandwiches for everyone, and hard, sweet little biscuits to eat with cheese made from goats' milk. Beowald ate with them, his face happy and contented. This was a great day in his life!

'Beowald, take us up to where we can see the Secret Forest,' begged Paul. 'Is it very far?'

'It will be two hours before we get there,' said the goatherd. He pointed with his hand, and it seemed to the children as if he must surely see, if he knew where to point. 'The way lies up there. It is steep and dangerous. But your ponies will take you safely.'

The children felt thrilled at the idea of seeing the Secret Forest from the summit of the mountain. They were very high up now, though the summit still seemed miles away. The air was cold and clear, and when the wind blew, the children wrapped their fur-lined cloaks around them. They could not imagine how Beowald could wear nothing but trousers.

When they had eaten all they could, they stood up. Ranni fetched the little ponies, who had been nibbling at the short grass growing where the mountainside was least rocky. The children sprang into the saddles and the ponies jerked their heads joyfully. Now, they thought, they were going back home!

But they were mistaken. Beowald led the way up a steep, rocky track that even goats might find difficult to tread.

'I can't think how Beowald knows the way,' called Peggy to Nora. 'There isn't a sign of any path, so far as I can see.'

'It's probably one that only the goats know,' said Ranni. 'See, that old goat with the great curling horns is before us. It almost looks as if he is leading the way!'

'Ah, my old one knows when I need him,' said the goatherd, and he put his flute to his mouth. He played a few merry little notes and the big goat came leaping lightly down to him. 'Stay by me, old one,' said Beowald.

The goat understood. He trotted in front of Beowald, and waited for him when he leapt up on to a rock. Beowald was as nimble as a goat himself, and it was amazing to the children to think that a blind youth should be so sure-footed. But then Beowald knew every inch of the mountainside.

Up they went and up. Sometimes the way was so steep that the ponies almost fell as they scrambled along, and sent crowds of stones rumbling down the mountainside. Ranni and Pilescu began to be doubtful about going farther. Ranni reined in his fat little pony.

'Beowald! Is the way much steeper?' he asked. 'This is dangerous for the children.'

'Ranni! It isn't!' cried Paul indignantly. 'I won't go back without seeing over the top. I won't!'

'We shall soon be there,' said Beowald, turning his dark eyes to Ranni. 'I can smell the forest already!'

The children all sniffed the air eagerly, but they could smell nothing. They wished they had the ears and nose of Beowald. He could not see, but he could sense many things that they could not.

They came to a narrow ledge and one by one the ponies went round it, pressing their bodies close against the rocky side of the mountain, for a steep precipice, with a fall of many hundreds of feet, was the other side! Nora and Peggy would not look, but the boys did not mind. It was exciting to be so high.

The old goat rounded the ledge first, and Beowald followed. 'We are here!' he called.

The ledge widened out round the bend – and the children saw that they were on the other side of Killimooin mountains! They were not right at the top of the mountain they were on, but had rounded a bend on the shoulder, and were now looking down on the thing they wanted so much to see – the Secret Forest!

'The Secret Forest! cried Paul, and Jack echoed his words.

'The Secret Forest! How big it is! How thick and dark! How high we are above it!'

All eight of them stared down into the valley that lay hidden and lost between the big ring of mountains. Only Beowald could not see the miles upon miles of dark green forest below, but his eyes seemed to rest on the valley below, just as the others did.

'Isn't it mysterious?' said Jack. 'It seems so still and quiet here. Even the wind makes no sound. I wish I could see that spire of smoke I thought I saw when we flew down low over the forest in the aeroplane.'

But there was no smoke to be seen, and no sound to be heard. The forest might have been dead for a thousand years, it was so still and lifeless.

'It's funny to stand here and look at the Secret Forest, and know you can't ever get to it,' said Mike. He looked down from the ledge he was standing on. There was a sheer drop down to the valley below, or so it seemed to the boy. It was quite plain that not even a goat could leap down.

'Now you can see why it is impossible to cross these mountains,' said Ranni. 'There is no way down the other side at all. All of them are steep and dangerous like this one. No man would dare to try his luck down that precipice, not even with ropes!'

The girls did not like looking down such a strange, steep precipice. They had climbed mountains before but none had been so steep as this one.

'I want to go back now,' said Nora. 'I'm feeling quite giddy.'

'It is time we all went,' said Ranni, looking at his watch. 'We must hurry too, or we shall be very late.'

'I can take you another way back,' said Beowald. 'It will be shorter for you to go to the castle. Follow me.'

With his goats around him, the blind youth began to leap down the mountainside. He was as sure-footed as the goats, and it was extraordinary to watch him. The ponies followed, slipping a little in the steep places. They were tired now, and were glad to be going home.

Down they all went and down. Nora gave a sudden shout that made the others jump. 'I can see Killimooin Castle. Hurrah! Another hour and we'll be home!'

They rounded a bend and then suddenly saw a strange place built into the rocky mountainside. They stopped and stared at it.

'What's that?' asked Paul. Ranni shook his head. He did not know and neither did Pilescu.

'It looks like some sort of temple,' said Nora, who remembered seeing pictures of stone temples in her history book. But this one was unusual, because it seemed to be built into the rock. There was a great half-broken archway, with roughly carved pillars each side.

'Beowald! Do you know what this place is?' asked Jack. The goatherd came back and stood beside Jack's pony.

'It is old, very old,' he said. 'It is a bad place. I think bad men once lived there, and were turned into stone for their wickedness. They are still there, for I have felt them with my hands.'

'What in the world does he mean?' said Peggy, quite frightened. 'Stone men! He's making it up!'

'Let's go and see,' said Jack, who was very seldom afraid of anything.

'No, thank you!' said the girls at once. But the boys badly wanted to see inside the strange, ruined old place. Beowald would not go with them. He stayed with the two girls.

'Come on. Let's see what these wicked stone men are!'

said Jack, with a grin. He dismounted from his pony, and passed through the great broken archway. It was dark inside the weird temple. 'Have you got a torch, Mike?' called Jack. Mike usually had a torch, a knife, string, and everything anyone could possibly want, somewhere about his person. Mike felt about and produced a torch.

He flashed it on – and the boys jumped in fright. Even Ranni and Pilescu jumped. For there, at the back of the temple-like cave, was a big stone man, seated on a low, flat rock!

'Oooh!' said Paul, and found Ranni's hand at once.

'It's an old statue!' said Jack, laughing at himself, and feeling ashamed of his sudden fright. 'Look – there are more, very broken and old. Aren't they odd? However did they get here?'

'Long, long ago the Baronians believed in strange gods,' said Ranni. 'These are probably stone images of them. This must be an ancient temple, forgotten and lost, known only to Beowald.'

'That sitting statue is the only one not broken,' said Jack. 'It's got a great crack down the middle of its body though – look. I guess one day it will fall in half. What a horrid face the stone man has got – sort of sneering.'

'They are very rough statues,' said Pilescu, running his hand over them. 'I have seen the same kind in other places in Baronia. Always they were in mountainside temples like this.'

'Let's go home!' called Nora, who was beginning to be very tired. 'What sort of stone men have you found? Come and tell us.'

'Only statues, cowardy custard,' said Jack, coming out of the ruined temple. 'You might just as well have seen them. Gee-up, there! Off we go!'

Off they went again, on the downward path towards Killimooin Castle, which could be seen very plainly now in the distance. In a short while Beowald said goodbye and disappeared into the bushes that grew just there. His goats followed him. The children could hear him playing on his flute, a strange melody that went on and on like a brook bubbling down a hill.

'I like Beowald,' said Nora. 'I'd like him for a friend. I wish he wasn't blind. I think it's marvellous the way he finds the path and never falls.'

The ponies trotted on and on, and at last came to the path that led straight down and round to the castle steps. Ranni took them to stable them, and Pilescu took the five tired children up the steps and into the castle.

They ate an enormous late tea, and then yawned so long and loud that Pilescu ordered them to bed.

'What, without supper!' said Paul.

'Your tea must be your supper,' said Pilescu. 'You are all nearly asleep. This strong mountain air is enough to send a grown man to sleep. Go to bed now, and wake refreshed in the morning.'

The children went up to bed. 'I'm glad we managed to see the Secret Forest,' said Jack. 'And that funny temple with those old stone statues. I'd like to see them again.'

He did – and had a surprise that was most unexpected!

CHAPTER NINE

Robbers!

A FEW days went by, days of wandering in the lower slopes of the mountain, looking for wild raspberries and watching the swift shy little animals that lived on the mountain. Yamen and Tooku told the children more tales, and nodded their heads when Jack told them of the ruined temple and the strange statues.

'Ah yes – it is very old. People do not go near it now because it is said that the statues come alive and walk at night.'

The children screamed with laughter at this. They thought some of the old superstitions were very funny. It seemed as if Yamen really believed in fairies and brownies, for always when she made butter, she put down a saucer of yellow cream by the kitchen door.

'It is for the brownie who lives in my kitchen!' she would say.

'But, Yamen, your big black cat drinks the cream, not the brownie,' Nora would say. But Yamen would shake her grey head and refuse to believe it.

Yamen used to go to buy what was needed at the village near the foot of the mountain each week. She had a donkey of her own, and Tooku had two of these sturdy little creatures. Tooku used sometimes to go with Yamen, and the third donkey would trot along behind them, with big baskets slung each side of his plump body, to bring back the many things Yamen bought for the household.

One day Yamen and Tooku started out with the third donkey behind them as usual. They set off down the track, and the children shouted goodbye.

'We shall be back in time to give you a good tea!' called Yamen. 'You shall have new-baked rusks with honey.'

But when teatime came there was no Yamen, no Tooku. Ranni and Pilescu looked out of the great doorway of the castle, puzzled. The two should be in sight, at least. It was possible to see down the track for a good way.

'I hope they haven't had an accident,' said Nora.

An hour went by, and another. The children had had their tea, and were wandering round the castle, throwing stones down a steep place, watching them bounce and jump.

'Look!' said Ranni, suddenly. Everyone looked down the track. One lone donkey was coming slowly along, with someone on his back, and another person stumbling beside him. Ranni ran to get a pony and was soon galloping along the track to find out what had happened.

The children waited anxiously. They were fond of Tooku and Yamen. As soon as the three climbed the steps of the castle, the children surrounded them.

'What's the matter, Yamen? Where are the other donkeys, Tooku? What have you done to your arm?'

'Aie, aie!' wept Yamen. 'The robbers came and took our goods and our donkeys! Tooku tried to stop them but they broke his arm for him. Aie-aie, what bad luck we have had this day! All the goods gone, and the two fine little donkeys!'

'They took all three,' said Tooku, 'but this one, my own good creature, must have escaped, for we heard him trotting after us as we hastened back home on foot.'

'What were the robbers like?' asked Jack.

'Strange enough,' answered Yamen. 'Small and wiry, with strips of wolf-skin round their middles. Each had a wolf's tail, dyed red, hanging behind him. Aie-aie, they were strange enough and fierce enough!'

'We heard tales in the town,' said Tooku, to Ranni and Pilescu. 'Many travellers have been robbed. These robbers take goods but not money. They come down from the mountains like goats, and they go back, no man knows where!'

'Have the villagers searched for their hiding

place?' asked Ranni. 'Have they hunted all about the mountainsides?'

'Everywhere!' said Yamen. 'Yes, not a place, not a cave has been forgotten. But nowhere is there a sign of the fierce robbers with their red wolves' tails!'

'Poor Yamen!' said Nora. The frightened woman was sitting in a chair, trembling. Pilescu bound up Tooku's arm. It was not broken, but badly gashed. The children felt very sorry.

Paul's mother soon heard of the disturbance and she was angry and upset. 'To think that such things should happen in Baronia!' she cried. 'I will send word to the King, and he shall send soldiers to search the mountainside.'

'The mountain-folk themselves have already done that,' said Ranni. 'If they have found nothing, the soldiers will find even less! It is a mystery where these men come from!'

'Perhaps they come from the Secret Forest!' said Jack. The others laughed at him.

'Idiot! Come from a place where nobody can go to!' said Mike.

'You children will not stir from this place without Ranni or Pilescu!' said Paul's mother.

'Madam, they have already promised not to,' said

Ranni. 'Do not be anxious. They are safe with us. We have always our revolvers with us.'

'I wish we hadn't come here now,' said the Queen, looking really worried. 'I wonder if we ought to go back. But I hear that it is hotter than ever in the big palace.'

The children had no wish to return when they heard that. 'We shall be quite safe here,' said Paul. 'The robbers will not dare to come anywhere near this castle, mother!'

'Silly child!' said his mother. 'Now that they know we are here, and that travellers will go to and fro, they will be all the more on the watch. They will haunt the road from here to the high road, and from here to the next village. I must get some more servants from the big palace. We must only go about in small companies, not alone.'

This was all very exciting. The boys talked about the robbers, and Mike felt three or four times an hour to see if his big scout-knife was safely in his broad belt. Paul thought of all the terrifying things he would do to the robbers if he caught them. Mike thought it would be marvellous to shut them all up in a cave somewhere. Jack pictured himself chasing the whole company down the mountainside.

The girls were not so thrilled, and were not much

impressed when the three boys promised to take care of them.

'What could you do against a company of robbers?' asked Nora.

'Well, this isn't the first time we've had adventures, and had to fight for safety,' said Mike, grandly.

'No, it's true we've had some exciting times and very narrow escapes,' said Peggy. 'But I don't particularly want to be chased and caught by robbers, even if you boys rescue me in the end!'

'Perhaps it's the stone men in the cave that come alive and rob people!' said Paul, with a grin.

'I'd like to go and have a look at those statues again,' said Jack. 'Ranni, can we go tomorrow? It's only about an hour's ride.'

'I don't want to go too far from the castle,' said Ranni. 'Well – we'll go as far as that old temple if you really want to. Though why you should want to see ancient statues, broken to pieces, when you've already seen them once is a puzzle to me!'

The children set off the next day to go to the old temple. They were on foot, as it really was not a great distance away, and Ranni said it would be good for them to walk. So up the mountain they trudged.

It was late afternoon when they started. They had

their tea with them. The sun shone down warmly and the children panted and puffed when they went up the hillside, so steep and stony.

'There's the old temple,' said Jack, at last, pointing to the ruined archway, hewn out of the mountain rock. 'It really is a funny place. It seems to be made out of a big cave, and the entrance is carved out of the mountain itself. Come on – let's go in and have another look. Nora, you come this time, and Peggy. You didn't come last time.'

'All right,' said Peggy. 'We'll come.'

They all went into the old temple, and switched on the torches they had brought. Once again they gazed on Beowald's 'stone men', and smiled to think of his idea that the statues had once been wicked men, turned into stone.

The biggest statue of all, at the back of the cave, sat on his wide flat rock, gazing with blank eyes out of the entrance. He seemed to be in much better repair than the others, who had lost noses, hands and even heads in some cases. Jack flashed his torch around, and suddenly came to a stop as he wandered around.

'Look here!' he said.

The others came to him and looked down at the ground, where his torch made a round ring of bright light. In the light was the print of a small bare foot. Jack swung his torch here and there, and on the floor of the temple other footprints could be seen – all small and bare, the toes showing clearly.

'Someone comes here quite a lot!' said Jack.

'More than one person,' said Mike, kneeling down and looking closely at a few prints with his torch. 'These are not the prints of the same person's feet. Look at this print here all the toes are straight – but this one has a crooked big toeprint. And that one is a little larger than the others.'

'It couldn't be Beowald's prints, could it?' asked Nora, remembering the bare feet of the goatherd.

'No. His feet are much bigger than those shown in these prints,' said Mike. 'I remember thinking what big feet he had.'

'Well – could it be the robbers' footprints?' cried Peggy, suddenly.

'It might be,' said Jack. 'But they are plainly not here – not living here, I mean! Anyway, they would be discovered easily enough if they did live here. Beowald would know.'

Ranni called the children. 'Come along. Tea is ready. We must hurry now, because it looks as if a mist is coming up.'

The children hurried out of the dark temple into the bright sunshine. They sat down to have their tea, telling Ranni and Pilescu what they had seen. But the two big Baronians were not much impressed.

'The prints are probably made by the feet of the

goatherds sent to search every nook and cranny of the mountainside, to look for the robbers' hiding place,' said Ranni.

This was disappointing. The children had quite made up their minds that they must belong to the robbers! Mike pointed down the hillside.

'Look at the clouds down there below us,' he said. 'They seem to be creeping up towards us.'

'They are,' said Pilescu, beginning to gather up the tea things. 'Come along. I don't want to get lost in a mountain mist!'

They all set off down the mountainside. Jack suddenly spied some juicy wild raspberries, and slipped off the path to get them. Before he had eaten more than a dozen he found himself surrounded by a thick grey mist!

'Blow!' said Jack, making his way back to the path. 'I can't even see the others now! Well, I know the path, that's one thing!'

He shouted, but could hear no answer. The others had gone round a bend, and could not hear him, though usually a shout in the mountains echoed round and round. But the thick mist muffled the sound, and Jack could hear no reply to his yell.

'I'll just go on and hope to catch the others up,' thought the boy. He set off, but after a while he had no idea of the right direction at all. The mist became thicker and thicker and the boy felt cold. He pulled his fur-lined cloak round him, and wondered what to do.

Something familiar about the rocky face of the mountain caught his eye. 'Well – look at that! I'm right back at the old temple!' said Jack, in astonishment. 'I've doubled back on the path somehow, and reached the temple-cave again. Well, I can't do better than shelter inside till the mist clears. Maybe it won't be long. They come and go very quickly.'

He went inside the cave where the old stone images were. He found a corner where he could sit, and he squatted down to wait. He yawned and shut his eyes. He hoped Ranni and Pilescu would not be very angry with him.

He dozed lightly, whilst the mist swirled round outside. He was awakened by the sound of voices, and sat up, expecting to see the other children coming into the temple to look for him. He half got up – and then sank back in the greatest astonishment.

The cave was full of strange, hoarse voices, speaking in the Baronian language, but using a broad country accent that Jack could not understand. It was dark there, and the boy could not see the people to whom the voices belonged. He dared not switch on his torch.

Then one of the men went to the entrance of the cave and

looked out, calling back that the mist was still there, but was clearing rapidly. Jack looked at him in amazement. He was small and wiry, and wore no clothes at all except for a strip of skin round his middle. The boy crouched back in his corner, suddenly scared.

The mist thinned outside the cave, and the man at the entrance was joined by others. They went out, and Jack saw that each man had a wolf's tail behind him, dyed red. They were the robbers!

There were many of them. Where had they come from? They had not been in the cave when the boy fell asleep, and if they had entered, he would have heard them. Where had they come from? There must be some secret entrance in the temple itself. But where could it be?

CHAPTER TEN

The Amazing Statue

THE CAVE was now empty. Jack got up cautiously and crept to the entrance. The mist was almost gone. Not a sign of the strange men was to be seen.

'They must have gone off to rob someone again!' thought the boy. 'I'll take a good look round the cave now I'm here and find out where those men came from. There *must* be some hidden entrance at the back. Possibly there's a big cave farther in, where they live. This is awfully exciting!'

But before he could put on his torch and look round he heard the sound of shouts outside.

'Jack! Jack! Where are you?'

It was Ranni's voice. Jack ran out of the old temple-cave. Ranni was some way down the mountain path. The boy shouted loudly.

'Ranni! I'm here, quite safe! I got lost in the mist.'

'Come along quickly, before the mist comes again!' ordered Ranni.

'But Ranni, wait! I've made a discovery!' yelled Jack.

'Come along at once,' shouted Ranni, sternly. 'Look at the mist coming up. It will be thicker this time. Come now, Jack.'

There was nothing for it but to go to Ranni. Jack leapt down the path, and as soon as he reached the big Baronian, he began to tell him what he had seen. But Ranni, anxious about the returning mist, paid little heed to the boy's excited chatter, and hurried him along as fast as he could go. Jack had no breath left to talk after a while, and fell silent. He could see that Ranni was cross with him.

The others had reached the castle safely. Ranni hurried Jack inside the door, just as the mist swirled up again, thick and grey.

'And now!' he said sternly, turning to Jack. 'Will you kindly tell me why you left us all? I had to go back and find you, and I might have hunted the mountainside for hours. I am not pleased with you, Jack.'

'I'm sorry, Ranni,' said Jack, humbly. 'I just went to pick some raspberries, that's all. Ranni, I saw the robbers!'

'I do not want to talk to you,' said Ranni. 'You have displeased me.' He went to his own room, leaving Jack behind.

Jack stared after the Baronian, rather hurt, and feeling decidedly small. He went to find the others.

'Jack! What happened to you?' cried Nora, rushing to him. 'We lost you, and Ranni went back.'

'I've some news,' said Jack, and his eyes gleamed. 'Strange news, too!'

'What?' cried everyone.

'I wandered about a bit, when the mist overtook me,' said Jack, 'and suddenly I found I was back at the old temple. So I went in out of the mist, and sat down to wait till it cleared. I dozed off for a bit – and suddenly I awoke and found the cave becoming full of voices! I heard more and more of them, and then a man went to the entrance of the cave and looked out – and it was one of the robbers!'

'Jack! Not really!' cried Peggy.

'Yes, really,' said Jack. 'When the mist cleared a bit, they all went out of the entrance, and I saw the wolves' tails they had, dyed red. They did look extraordinary.'

'Did they come into the cave to shelter then?' asked Mike.

'No – that's the funny part,' said Jack. 'They didn't! I feel absolutely certain that they came into the cave by some secret way – perhaps at the back of the temple. I believe there must be a big cave further in, where they live.'

'So those footprints we saw must be theirs, after all,' said Paul. 'Oh, Jack – this is awfully exciting, isn't it! What did Ranni say when you told him?'

'He wouldn't listen,' said Jack. 'He was angry with me.'

'Well, he'll soon be all right again,' said Paul, cheerfully. 'Ranni's temper never lasts long. I know that.'

Paul was right. Ranni forgot his anger in a very short time, and when he came into the children's room, he was his usual smiling self. The boys went to him at once.

'Ranni! We know where the robbers hide!'

'Ranni, do listen, please. Jack saw the robbers.'

This time Ranni did listen, and what he heard made him call Pilescu at once. The two men were eager to hear every word that Jack had to tell.

'It looks as if we shall be able to round up the robbers quickly now,' said Ranni. 'Good! You must be right, Jack – there is probably a secret entrance somewhere in the cave, leading from a big cave farther in.'

'We must make a search as quickly as possible,' said Pilescu. 'Ranni, the moon is full tonight. You and I will take our most powerful torches and will examine that temple from top to bottom tonight!'

'Oh, Pilescu, let me come too,' begged Jack.

'And me!' cried Mike and Paul together.

Pilescu shook his big head. 'No – there may be danger. You must stay safely here in the castle.'

Jack was angry. 'Pilescu! It was *my* discovery! Don't be mean. You *must* take me with you. Please!'

'You will not come,' said Pilescu, firmly. 'We are responsible for your safety in Baronia, and you will not be allowed to run into any danger. Ranni and I will go tonight, and tomorrow you shall hear what we have found.'

The two men went out of the room, talking together. Jack stared after them fiercely. The boy was almost in tears.

'It's too bad,' he said. 'It *was* my discovery! And they're going to leave me out of it. I didn't think Ranni and Pilescu would be so mean.'

The boy was hurt and angry. The others tried to comfort him. Jack sat and brooded for a little while and then he suddenly made up his mind.

'I shall go, too!' he said to the others, in a low tone. 'I shall follow them and see what they find. I won't miss this excitement.'

'But you promised not to go out alone,' said Mike, at once. All the children thought the world of their promises and never broke one.

'Well, I *shan't* be alone – I shall be with Ranni and Pilescu, and they won't know it!' grinned Jack, quite good-tempered again now that he had thought of a way to join in the adventure. For adventure it had become, there wasn't a doubt of that!

The others laughed. It was quite true. Jack would certainly not be alone!

So, that night, after they had gone to bed, Jack kept his ears pricked to listen to any sounds of Ranni and Pilescu leaving. The moon swam up into the sky and the mountainside was as light as day. The boy suddenly heard the low voices of the two Baronians, and he knew they were going down the passage to make their way to the great front door.

He had not undressed, so he was ready to follow them. After them he went, as quietly as a cat. The others whispered to him:

'Good luck!'

'Don't let Ranni see you or you'll get a ticking-off!'

'Look after yourself, Jack!'

The big front door opened, and shut quietly. Jack waited for a moment, opened it, and crept after the two men. He had to be careful to keep well in the black shadows, for it was easy to see anyone in the moonlight.

Up the mountain track behind the castle went Ranni and Pilescu. They did not speak, and they made as little noise as they could. They kept a sharp look-out for any sign of the robbers, but there was none. Word had come to the castle that evening that a company of local people, returning from market, had been set upon and robbed that afternoon, and the two Baronians had no doubt that the robbers were the men that Jack had seen in the cave.

'If we can find the entrance to their lair, we can get soldiers up here, and pen the whole company in, and catch them one by one as they come out,' said Ranni, in a low tone. Pilescu nodded. He heard a sound, and stopped.

'What is it?' whispered Ranni.

'Nothing,' answered Pilescu, after a pause. 'I thought I heard something.'

He had! He had heard the fall of a stone dislodged by Jack, who was following them as closely as he dared! The boy stopped when Pilescu stopped, and did not move again until the two men went forward.

In about an hour's time they were at the old temple. The moon shone in at the ruined entrance. Ranni gave a startled exclamation as he went in, for the moon shone full on the face of the old stone image at the back. It seemed very lifelike!

'Now,' said Ranni, flashing his torch round the cave. 'You take a look that side and I'll take this. Examine every inch of the rock.'

The moon suddenly went behind a big cloud and the world went dark. Jack took the chance of slipping into the cave without the two men seeing him. He thought he could hide behind the images, as the men worked round the cave. He stood behind one near the entrance and watched Ranni and Pilescu examining the rocky wall, trying to find some hidden entrance to another cave beyond.

'I can find nothing,' said Pilescu, in a low voice.

Jack stood behind the statue and watched, hoping that one of the men would discover something. How he wished he could help too – but he was afraid of showing himself in case Ranni was angry again.

He stared at the big squatting statue at the back of the cave. The moon had come out again and was shining full on the image. As Jack watched, a very strange thing began to happen!

The statue's face began to widen! It began to split in half! Jack stared in astonishment and horror. What could be happening? Was it coming alive? Were those old tales true, then?

Then he saw that the whole statue was splitting slowly and silently in half. The two halves were moving apart. It all happened so smoothly and silently that Ranni and Pilescu heard no sound at all, and had no warning.

Jack was so amazed that he could not say a word. The statue split completely in half, the two halves moving right apart – and then, from the floor of the flat rock beneath, a man's shaggy head appeared, full in the moonlight – the head of one of the robbers!

Jack gave a yell. 'Ranni! Pilescu! Look out! The robbers are coming! Look at the statue!'

Ranni and Pilescu, amazed at Jack's voice, and at what he said, swung round quickly. They stared in the utmost amazement at the split statue, and saw the head and shoulders of the robber below. With a wild yell the robber leapt up into the temple, calling to his friends below:

'Come! Come! Here are enemies!'

In half a minute the cave was full of robbers. Ranni and Pilescu, taken completely by surprise, had their hands bound. They fought and struggled fiercely, but the robbers were too many for them.

Ranni remembered Jack's voice, and knew that the boy must be somewhere about. He must have followed them! Ranni called out in English:

'Don't show yourself, Jack. Go and give warning to the others.'

Jack did not answer, of course. He crouched down behind a statue, watching the fight, knowing that it would be useless to join in, and hoping that the robbers would not see him.

Before his astonished eyes, the boy saw the wolf-tailed men force the two Baronians down through the hole beneath the great statue. Every robber followed. Then the statue, smoothly and silently as before, began to move. The two halves joined together closely, and the image was whole once more, its cracked face shining in the moonlight.

'No wonder there was such a crack down the middle of it!' thought the boy. 'It wasn't a crack – it was a split, where the two halves joined! Golly, this is awful. I wonder if it's safe to go.'

He waited for a while and then stole quietly out of the cave, looking behind him fearfully as he went. But no robber was there to follow him. The boy sped swiftly down the track in the moonlight, anxious to get to the others.

They were all awake. Jack got them into his room and told them hurriedly all that had happened. Paul was shocked, and anxious to hear about Ranni and Pilescu, whom he loved with all his heart.

'I am going to rescue them,' he announced, getting into his clothes at once.

'Don't be an idiot, Paul,' said Mike. 'You can't go after robbers.'

'Yes, I can,' said Paul, fiercely, and his big dark eyes gleamed. 'I am a Baronian prince, and I will not leave my men in danger. I go now to find them!'

When Paul got ideas of this sort into his head, there was no stopping him. Jack groaned. He turned to the girls.

'We'd better go with Paul and keep the idiot out of danger. You go and wake Tooku and Yamen and tell them what has happened. They will think of the best thing to do. Don't frighten Paul's mother, will you?'

Paul was already out of the front door, running down the steps in the moonlight. Ranni and Pilescu were in danger! Then he, their little prince must rescue them. Mike and Jack tore after him. A big adventure had begun!

CHAPTER ELEVEN

The Beginning of the Adventure

MIKE AND Jack soon caught up with Paul. The boy was struggling up the steep track as fast as he could go. He had no clear idea as to exactly what he was going to do. All he knew was that he meant to find Ranni and Pilescu and rescue them from the robbers.

'Paul! You're going the wrong way,' panted Jack, as he came up to Paul. 'You really are an idiot. You'd be lost in the mountains if we hadn't come after you. Look – you go this way, not the one you're taking.'

Paul was glad to have the others with him. He pulled his fur-lined cloak around him, for he was cold. The others were wearing theirs too. They climbed steadily up the mountainside, the moon showing them the way quite clearly. Mike hoped that clouds would not blow up, for it would be impossible to find their way in the dark. He thought of Beowald, the blind goatherd. He did not mind the dark. It made no difference to him at all!

Up they went and up, and an hour went by. Paul did not seem to be at all tired, though Jack's legs ached badly.

But then he had already been to the temple-cave and back once before that night!

They came near the cave, and trod softly, keeping to the shadows, in case any of the robbers should be about. Suddenly a figure showed itself from behind a rock! Quick as lightning Jack pulled the other two down beside him in a big shadow, and the three of them crouched there, their hearts beating painfully. Was it a robber, left on guard? Had he seen them?

The moon went behind a small cloud and the mountainside lay in darkness. Jack strained his eyes and ears to find out if the night-wanderer was anywhere near.

Then he heard the plaintive notes of the little flute that Beowald played! It must be the goatherd, wandering at night as he so often did.

'Beowald!' called Jack, softly. 'Where are you?'

The moon sailed out from behind the cloud and the boys saw the goatherd seated on a nearby rock, his head turned towards them.

'I am here,' he said. 'I heard you. I knew you were friends. What are you doing up here at night?'

Jack came out from his hiding place. He told Beowald in a few words all that had happened. The goatherd listened in amazement.

'Ah, so that is why I thought the stone men came to life

at night!' he said. 'It was robbers I heard coming forth from the temple, and not the stone men. There must be a deep cave below the floor of the temple. I will come with you to find it.'

The goatherd led the way to the cave. The moon went in again behind a cloud, and the boys were glad to be with Beowald for the last piece of their climb. They could not have found their way otherwise. But darkness did not matter to the blind youth. He found his way as surely as if he were seeing the path in daylight!

They came near to the temple, treading very cautiously. Not a sound was to be heard. 'We'd better creep into the cave whilst the moon is behind a cloud,' whispered Jack. 'Paul, ask Beowald if he thinks any robbers are about now. His ears are so sharp that surely he would know.'

Paul whispered to Beowald in the Baronian language. The goatherd shook his head. 'There is no one near,' he said. 'I have heard nothing at all, and my ears would tell me if a robber was in the cave. I should hear him breathing.'

The boys crept silently into the dark cave. When they were in, the moon shone out and lighted up the strange stone face of the big statue at the back. It seemed to look sneeringly at the three boys.

Jack went up to the image, and ran his fingers down the crack that he had seen widen into a split when the statue divided into halves. He wondered how he could find out the working of the strange image. There must be some way of opening it, both from above and below. What was it? He must find it, or he would not be able to find the place where the robbers had taken Ranni and Pilescu.

But no matter how he felt and pushed and pulled, the crack remained a crack, and did not widen into a split. The other two boys tried as well, but they had no more success than Jack. They looked at one another in despair.

'Let my fingers try,' said the voice of Beowald. 'My eyes cannot see, but my fingers can. They can feel things that only the whiskers of a mouse could sense!'

This was perfectly true. The blind youth's fingers were so sensitive that they could tell him more than the eyes of others could tell them. The boys watched Beowald run his fingers down the crack in the middle of the statue. They watched him feel round the staring stone eyes. They followed his quivering fingers round the neck and head, touching, feeling, probing, almost like the feelers of an enquiring butterfly!

Suddenly Beowald's sensitive fingers found something and they stopped. The boys looked at him.

'What is it, Beowald?' whispered Prince Paul.

'The statue is not solid just here,' answered the goatherd. 'Everywhere else it is solid, made of stone – but just behind here, where its right ear is, it is hollow.'

'Let me feel,' said Jack eagerly, and pushed away the goatherd's fingers. He placed his own behind the right ear of the statue, but he could feel nothing at all. The stone felt just as solid to him there as anywhere else. The other boys felt as well, but to them, as to Jack, the stone was solid there. How could Beowald's fingers know whether stone was solid or hollow behind a certain spot? It seemed like magic.

Beowald put his fingers back again on the spot he had found. He moved them about, pressed and probed. But nothing happened. Jack shone his torch on to the ear. He saw that it was cleaner than the rest of the head, as if it had been handled a good deal. It occurred to him that the ear itself might be the place containing a spring or lever that worked the statue so that it split in half.

The left ear was completely solid, Jack saw – but the right ear, on the contrary, had a hole in it, as have human ears! Beowald found the hole at the same time as Jack saw it, and placed his first finger inside it. The tip of his finger touched a rounded piece of metal set inside the ear. Beowald pushed against it – and a lever was set in motion that split the stone image silently into half!

Actually it was a very simple mechanism, but the boys did not know that. They stared open-mouthed as the statue split completely down the crack, and the two halves moved smoothly apart. Beowald knew what was happening, though he could not see it. He was afraid, and moved back quickly. He half thought the statue was coming alive, when it moved!

'Look – there's a hole underneath the statue, in the middle of the low rock it sits on,' said Jack, and he shone his torch down it. The hole was round in shape, and would take a man's body easily. A rope, made of strips of leather, hung down the hole from a staple at the top.

'That's the entrance to the robber's lair!' said Jack, in a low voice. 'No doubt about that! I bet their cave is below this one, in the mountain itself.'

'I'm going to see,' said the little prince, who seemed that night to be more than a small boy. He was a prince, he was growing up to be a king, he was Lord of Baronia, he was going to take command and give orders! Jack pulled him back as he was about to go down into the dark hole.

'Wait! We might all fall into a trap. Don't do anything silly. We shan't help Ranni and Pilescu by being foolish.'

'I will go to rouse the local people and to bring help,' said Beowald. 'I would like to come with you, but I am no good in a strange place. My feet, my ears and my hands only help me when I am on my mountainside. In a strange place I am lost.'

'We will go down the hole and find out what we can,' said Jack. 'You get the others and follow us as soon as you are able to. The girls will have told Tooku and Yamen by now, and maybe they will be on the way here with one or two of the servants. I expect Paul's mother will send for some soldiers, too.'

Beowald did not understand all that Jack said, for the boy did not speak the Baronian language very well as yet. Paul quickly translated for him, and Beowald nodded his head.

'Do not fall into the hands of the robbers,' he said. 'Why do you not wait here until I come back?'

'I go to rescue my men,' said Prince Paul haughtily. 'Where they go, I follow.'

'You must do as you wish,' said the goatherd. Jack slid down into the hole, and took hold of the rope. He went down and down, whilst Mike shone his torch on to him. Beowald waited patiently, seeing nothing, but knowing by his ears all that was happening.

The hole went down for a long way. Jack swung on the rope, his arms getting tired. Then he found that there were rough ledges here and there on the sides of the hole, on which he could rest his feet now and again, to relieve his arms.

The hole came to an end at last. Jack felt his toes

touching ground once more. He let go the rope and felt round with his hands. He could feel nothing. The hole must have come out into some kind of cave. The boy could hear no sound of any sort, and he thought it would be safe to switch on his torch.

He switched it on, and saw that, as he had imagined, he was in a cave, through the roof of which the hole showed, dark and round. 'I wonder if this is the robbers' lair,' thought the boy, flashing the torch around. But there was nothing at all in the rocky cave, whose rugged walls threw back the gleam of the torch.

Mike's feet appeared at the bottom of the hole and the boy jumped down beside Jack. Then came Paul. They all stood together, examining the cave.

'It doesn't look as if anyone lives here at all,' said Mike. 'There are no beds where you might expect the robbers to sleep, not a sign of any pot or pan. I don't believe this is their lair.'

'Well, what is it, then?' demanded Jack. 'I saw them go down here, didn't I? Goodness knows how Ranni and Pilescu were taken down, with their hands tied! Where can they be?'

'They're nowhere here at all,' said Paul, flashing his torch into every corner. 'It's odd. What can have become of them?'

It really was a puzzle. Jack began to go round the little cave, his footsteps echoing in a weird way. He flashed his torch up and down the walls, and suddenly came to a stop.

'Here's another way out!' he said. 'Look! It's quite plain to see. I'm surprised we didn't see it before when we shone our torches round.'

The boys looked. They saw that halfway up the opposite wall of the cave was a narrow opening. They jumped on to a ledge and peered through it. It was plain that it led out of the cave, and was a passage through the rock.

'Come on,' said Jack. 'This is the way the robbers must have gone. I'll go first!'

He was soon in the passage that led from the cave. He flashed his torch in front of him. The way was dark and rough, and the passage curved as it went, going downwards all the time. Where in the world did it lead to!

CHAPTER TWELVE

The River in the Mountain

AS THE boys crept down the rocky passage, they suddenly heard a curious noise in the distance. They stopped.

'What's that noise?' asked Jack. It was a kind of rumbling, gurgling sound, sometimes loud and sometimes soft. The boys listened.

'I don't know,' said Mike, at last. 'Come on. Maybe we shall find out.'

On they went again, and very soon they discovered what the strange noise was. It was made by water! It was a waterfall in the mountain, a thing the children had not even thought of! They came out into a big cave, and at one end fell a great stream of water. The cave was damp and cold, and the boys shivered.

They went over to the curious waterfall. 'I suppose the snow melts on the top of the mountain and the water finds its way down here,' said Jack, thoughtfully. 'It must run through a rocky passage, something like the one we have just been in, and then, when the passage ends, the water tumbles down with that rumbling noise. I'm quite wet with the spray!'

The water fell steadily from a hole in the roof of the cave, where, as Jack said, there must be a tunnel or passage down which the water ran before it fell into the cave.

'Where does the water go to, I wonder?' said Mike. 'It rushes off into that tunnel, look – and becomes a kind of river going through the mountain. I think it's weird. I wonder if the robbers live in *this* cave – but there still seems to be no sign of them or their belongings. After all, if people live somewhere, even in a cave, they scatter a few belongings about!'

But there was nothing at all to be seen, and, as far as the boys could see, no way of getting out of the 'waterfall cave,' as they called it.

They wandered round, looking for some outlet – but the water seemed to have found the only outlet – the tunnel down which it rushed after falling on to the channeled floor of the cave.

The boys went back to the water and gazed at it. Jack saw that through hundreds of years the waterfall had worn itself a bed or channel on the floor of the cave, and that only the surface water overflowed on to the ground where the boys stood. The channel took the main water, and it rushed off down a tunnel, and then was lost to sight in the darkness.

'I suppose the robbers couldn't possibly have gone down that tunnel, could they?' said Paul suddenly. 'There isn't a ledge or anything they could walk on, is there, going beside that heaving water?'

The boys tried to see through the spray that was flung up by the falling water. Jack gave a shout.

'Yes – there *is* a ledge, and I believe we could get on to it. For goodness' sake be careful not to fall into that churning water! We'd be carried away and drowned if so, it's going at such a pace!'

The boy bent down, ran through the flying spray, and leapt on to a wet ledge beside the water, just inside the tunnel into which it disappeared. He nearly slipped and fell, but managed to right himself.

He flashed his torch into the tunnel and saw the amazing sight of the heaving, rushing water tearing away down the dark vault of the mountain tunnel. It was very weird, and the noise inside the tunnel was frightening.

Paul and Mike were soon beside Jack. He shouted into their ears. 'We'd better go along here and see if it leads anywhere. I think this is the way the robbers must have gone with Ranni and Pilescu. Keep as far from the water as you can and don't slip, whatever you do!'

THE RIVER IN THE MOUNTAIN

The boys made their way with difficulty along the water-splashed tunnel. The water roared beside them in its hollowed-out channel. The noise was thunderous. Their feet were soon wet with the splashing of the strange river.

'The tunnel is widening out here,' shouted back Jack, after about an hour. 'Our ledge is becoming almost a platform!'

So it was. After another minute or two the boys found themselves standing on such a broad ledge that when they crouched against the back of it, the spray from the river no longer reached them.

They rested there for a while. Paul was terribly tired by now. Mike looked at his watch. It was four o'clock in the morning! The sun would be up outside the mountain – but here it was as dark as night.

'I feel so sleepy,' said Paul, cuddling up against Mike. 'I think we ought to have a good long rest.'

Jack got up and looked around the broad platform for a more comfortable resting-place. He gave a shout that quickly brought the others to him.

'Look,' said Jack, shining his torch on to a recess in the wall of the tunnel at the back of the platform. 'This is where the robbers must sometimes rest before going on to wherever they live!'

In the recess, which was like a broad shelf of rock, lay some fur rugs. The boys cuddled into them, snuggled up to one another, closed their eyes and fell asleep at once. They were tired out with their night's travel.

They slept for some hours, and then Jack awoke with a start. He opened his eyes and remembered at once where he was – on the inside of the mountain! He sat up – and suddenly saw the platform outside the recess where the boys were, was lighted brightly. Voices came to him – and he saw a flaring torch held high. What could be happening now?

The other boys did not wake. They were too tired to hear a sound! Jack leaned out of the rugs and tried to see who was holding the torch. He had a nasty shock – for it was held by one of the robbers! When Jack saw him turn round and his red wolf tail swing out behind him, he knew without a doubt that the robbers were there within a few feet of him.

The boy tried to see what they were doing. They were at the edge of the river, at the end of the rocky platform. As Jack watched he saw two more men come up from the ledge that ran beside the river. It was plain that the broad platform they were on narrowed into the same sort of ledge that ran beside the upper part of the river. The men were coming up from lower down – and they were dragging something behind them, something that floated on the water. Jack could not see what it was, for the light from the torch flickered and shook, making shadows dance over everything.

The men called to one another hoarsely. They did something at the edge of the water, and then, without a glance toward the recess in which the boys were sleeping, they turned and made their way up the tunnel through which the boys had come, keeping along the ledge in single file. They were going up to the temple-cave, Jack was sure.

'Going to rob people again, I suppose!' thought the boy, excitedly. 'They've taken Ranni and Pilescu somewhere further down, and tied them up, I expect – left them safe, as they thought. Golly, if only we could find out where they are, we could rescue them easily now that the robbers have left them for awhile.'

He looked at his watch. It showed ten minutes to nine! It was morning. Would Yamen and Tooku, Beowald and the villagers have arrived at the temple-cave yet, and meet the robbers on their way? Jack could not imagine what would happen. He woke the others and told them what he had seen.

'The thing to do now is to get along as quickly as we can, and find out where Ranni and Pilescu are,' he said. 'The robbers have gone in the opposite direction. Come on, I saw where they came from. It's plain they follow the river.'

The boys shook off the warm rugs. Jack flashed his torch round the comfortable recess to make sure they had left nothing behind. The light fell on a tiny shelf at the back. In it was something wrapped in a cloth. Jack unwrapped it in curiosity. Inside was a big Baronian loaf, crusty and stale.

'We'd better soak it in water and eat some,' said Jack, pleased. 'I'm hungry enough to enjoy bread and water, even if you two aren't! I suppose the robbers leave bread here to help themselves to when they rest in these rugs.'

When they pulled off the crust of the big loaf they found that the bread was not too hard to eat after all. They did not even need to soak it in water. Paul, as usual, had a big packet of the honey-flavoured Baronian chocolate with him, and the three boys thoroughly enjoyed their strange meal beside the rushing mountain river.

There was a flattish sort of cup on the little shelf where they had found the bread, and the boys dipped this into the clear river water and drank. It was as cold as ice, and tasted delicious.

Jack bent down to fill the cup again and something caught his eye, as he flashed his torch round. He stopped and gave a surprised exclamation.

'Whatever's that? Look – that thing over there?'

The others looked. Tied by a leather thong to a jutting rock was what looked like a hollowed-out raft. It was broad and flat, with a hollow in the middle. The sides were strengthened with strip upon strip of leather, bound tightly over the edges.

'It's a raft-boat, or boat-raft, whatever you like to call it!' said Mike, surprised. 'I've never seen anything like it before. Isn't it odd? What's it for?'

'To go down the river, I imagine!' said Jack, joyfully. 'My word, we shall soon get along if we use that raft!'

'But how did the men get here on it?' said Paul, puzzled. 'They couldn't float against the current, and it's very strong here.'

'They probably crept up on the narrow rocky ledge that seems to run beside the river all the way,' said Jack. 'But behind them each time they come, they must drag a raft like this, which they use to get themselves back quickly. I say, this is getting awfully exciting! We can take the raft for ourselves, and that will mean that we leave the robbers I saw just now far behind us, for they will have to walk along the ledge as we did, instead of using their boat. Come on – let's try it!'

'I shouldn't be surprised if it takes us right to the place where Ranni and Pilescu are prisoners,' said Paul. 'Undo that leather thong, Mike, and let's get into the funny boat.'

The boys untied the leather strip, and got into the hollow centre of the solid raft. It was absolutely unsinkable, made out of wood from a big tree, hollowed out carefully in the middle. The boys soon found out why the edges were bound so thickly and firmly with strips of leather!

They let the raft go free on the rushing stream. At once they floated into the dark tunnel from which Jack had seen the robbers come. The raft swung round and round as it went, and bumped hard against the rocky sides of the strange dark tunnel. The leather edges took off the worst jolts, but even so, the boys had to cling tightly to the raft to prevent themselves from being jerked overboard!

'This is the most exciting thing we've ever done!' shouted Jack, above the roar of the water. 'Golly, aren't we going fast! I hope we don't come to a waterfall!'

Down they went on the rushing mountain river, down and down in the darkness. The raft rushed along as fast as a speed boat, and the three boys gasped for breath. Where did the river flow to?

CHAPTER THIRTEEN

In the Secret Forest

THE RAFT rushed along, swinging and bobbing. Sometimes the water was smoother, and then the raft floated more slowly, but on the whole it rushed along at a terrific pace. Once the roof of the tunnel was so low that the boys had to crouch right down on the raft to prevent their heads being bumped hard against it.

'We're going down and down,' said Jack. 'The river must be running right through the mountain in a downward direction, and I suppose will come out at the other side.'

'The other side! Do you mean where the Secret Forest is?' cried Mike.

Jack nodded his head and his eyes gleamed eagerly in the light of Mike's torch. 'Yes! If the river *does* come out into the open, and I suppose it must at last, we shall be somewhere on the mountainside overlooking the Secret Forest itself. So, you see, there is a way of getting there! And the robbers know it. I shouldn't be surprised if that really was smoke I saw that day we flew over it in the aeroplane.'

The boys felt even more excited, if that was possible! They sat on the weird raft-boat and thought about their night's adventure. It was stranger than any they had ever had. This mountain river seemed never-ending. How long did it go on and on?

After about two hours a startling thing happened. Jack saw a light, bright and golden, far ahead of them. 'Look!' he said. 'What's that?'

They floated rapidly nearer and nearer to the gleam, and soon they saw what it was. It was daylight, sunlight, bright and golden. They were soon coming out into the open air!

'We'll be able to get off the raft and stretch our legs a bit! said Jack, thankfully, for they were all beginning to feel very cramped indeed. But Jack was wrong. There was no getting off that raft yet!

It suddenly shot out into the open air, and the boys blinked their eyes, dazzled by the sudden bright sunshine. When they could see properly, they saw that they were indeed on the other side of the steep Killimooin mountains!

Below them, not very far away, was the Secret Forest! The mountain river, after having flowed for miles through the mountain tunnels, was now flowing down the slopes of the hill, taking the raft with it. It spread out into a wide river, and the raft sailed along in the middle, where the current was swift and strong. There appeared to be no dangerous waterfall to navigate! That was very fortunate, Jack thought.

'Do you suppose this river goes right down to the Secret Forest?' said Mike, trying to see where it flowed, far ahead of them. He caught glimpses of silver here and there, near the forest. It really did look as if the river flowed to it!

'I believe it does,' said Jack, as the raft floated swiftly down the current. 'We are getting nearer and nearer!'

After some time the river was very near to the great forest. The boys could see how wide and thick and dark it was. Now it no longer looked merely a great stretch of green; they could see the trees themselves, tall and close-set together. The river flowed on and on towards it.

The raft reached the outermost fringe of trees, and the river then disappeared into the forest. The boys were swept along on the raft, and as soon as they entered the forest, the sunshine disappeared, and a dim green light was all they had to see by.

'How dark and thick the trees are!' said Jack, awed. 'The river must go right through this forest.'

'I wonder where it goes to,' said Mike. 'Rivers all go to the sea. How can this one get out of this closed-in valley?

You would think it would make a big lake – all this water flowing down the mountainside like this, with nowhere to escape to!'

This was a puzzle, too. The boys thought about it as the raft swung along beneath the arching trees. Then, quite suddenly, they were in a big, wide pool, like a small lake, completely surrounded by trees. The river flowed through the pool, and out at the opposite side.

The raft swung to the side of the pool, and Jack gave a cry of surprise.

'This is where the robbers live! Look at those strange houses, or whatever you like to call them!'

The boys saw that round the lakeside were strange, beehive-shaped houses, made of branches of trees and dried mud. From a hole at the top smoke appeared. Then Jack knew that he had been right when he thought he had seen a spiral of smoke from the aeroplane! The smoke from the beehive houses joined together as it rose into the air, and made a straight streak of blue smoke that hung almost motionless, for no wind came into that still valley.

No one was to be seen. If there was anyone in the huts, they must be sleeping, Jack thought! Their raft swung silently to the bank and the three boys leapt off at once. They crouched down in the bushes watching to see if anyone had noticed them. But nobody had. Not a soul appeared from the curious huts.

The boys were very hungry indeed, but they dared not go to ask for food. They whispered together, wondering what to do. Behind them was the deep, dark forest. In front was the great pool, out of which flowed the river, disappearing into the depths of the Secret Forest.

'Do you suppose all the robbers have gone up to the temple-cave?' whispered Mike. Jack shook his head. 'No,' he said. 'I only saw five or six. Hundreds must live here. Sh! Look, there are some children!'

The boys saw four or five children coming from the forest, going towards the huts. They had nothing on at all, except for a strip of skin round their waists. They were dirty, and their bright hair was tangled and long. They wore bright bird feathers behind their ears, and looked real little ruffians.

A woman appeared at the door of one hut, and the children shouted to her. Paul turned to the others.

'Did you understand what those children said? They said they had been to see the big men who were prisoners! So Ranni and Pilescu must be here somewhere. Shall we try going along that path where the children came from?'

'We should get completely lost in the Secret Forest,' said Mike, feeling scared. 'There are probably wolves here too. I almost wish we hadn't come. We should have waited and come with the others!'

'We will go down the forest path,' said Paul, suddenly becoming the Prince of Baronia again. 'Stay here if you do not wish to follow me. I, myself, will find Ranni and Pilescu!'

There was nothing for it but to follow Paul. He skirted the pool carefully and then found the narrow path down which the robber-children had come. It ran between the thickly growing trees, and was evidently much used. Here and there the trees were curiously marked as if with an axe.

'Perhaps it's the way the robbers have of marking their way through the forest,' said Paul.

'Yes – sort of signposts,' answered Jack, who had thought the same thing. 'Well, as long as I see those marks, I shan't feel lost!'

They went on down the narrow, twisting path. It curved round trees, wandered between the thick trunks, and seemed never-ending. Now and again the children saw the axe marks on a tree trunk again. The forest was very quiet and still. No wind moved the branches of the trees. No bird sang. It was very mysterious and silent.

Jack's sharp ears heard the sound of voices. 'Someone's coming!' he said. 'Shin up a tree, quick!'

The three chose trees that did not seem too difficult to climb quickly. They were up them in a trice. A squirrel-like animal bounded away in alarm from Jack. The boy peered down between the branches.

He saw three more children going along, fortunately towards the pool they had left. They shouted to one another, and seemed to be playing some sort of hopping game. They soon passed, and did not guess that there were three pairs of anxious eyes following their movements from the branches above them.

As soon as the robber-children were out of sight the boys jumped down and went on again. 'I hope that they haven't hidden Ranni and Pilescu too far away!' said Jack, with a groan. 'I'm getting tired again and awfully hungry!'

'So am I,' said Mike. Paul said nothing. He meant to go on until he found his men. He did not seem to be tired, though he looked it. Jack thought he was a very plucky boy indeed, for he was younger and smaller than the other two, and yet managed to keep up with them very well.

Jack stopped again and motioned to the others to listen. They stood still, and heard voices once more. Up a tree they went at once, but this time the voices did not come any nearer. Paul suddenly went red with excitement. He leaned towards Jack, who was on the branch next to him.

'Jack! I think that is Pilescu's deep voice. Listen!'

They all listened, and through the forest came the deep tones of Pilescu's voice, without a doubt. In a trice the boys had shinned down the tree again and were running down the path towards the voices.

They came out into a small clearing. In the middle of this there was a hole, or what looked like a hole from where the boys stood. Across the top of the hole were laid heavy beams of wood, separated each from the other by a few inches, to allow air to penetrate into the hole.

It was from this hole or pit that the voices came. Mike took a quick look round the clearing to see if anyone was there. But it seemed to be completely empty. He ran across to the pit.

'Ranni! Pilescu?' he cried, and Paul tried to force apart the heavy logs of wood.

'Ranni! Are you there? Pilescu, are you hurt?' cried Paul, in a low voice.

There was an astonished silence, and then came Ranni's voice, mingled with Pilescu's.

'Paul! Little lord! What are you doing here? Paul, can it be you?'

'Yes – I'm here and Mike and Jack,' said Paul. 'We have come to rescue you.'

'But how did you get here?' cried Ranni, in amazement. 'Did you come through the mountain and down the river into the depths of the Secret Forest?'

'Yes,' said Mike. 'It has been a tremendous adventure, I can tell you.'

'Are you all all right?' asked Pilescu.

'Yes, except that we're awfully hungry,' said Jack, with a laugh.

'If you can move those logs, with our help, we will give you food,' said Ranni. 'We have some here in this pit. The robbers put bread and water here, and we have plenty. Goodness knows what they meant to do with us. I suppose they captured us because they knew we had found the secret of their coming and going, and did not want us to tell anyone.'

The boys began to try and move the heavy logs. Ranni and Pilescu helped them. They shifted little by little, though it was as much as the whole five of them could do to move them even an inch! At last, however, there was enough space for Ranni and Pilescu to squeeze out of the pit, and haul themselves up on to the level ground.

They sat there panting. 'Not a nice prison at all,' said Ranni, jokingly, as he saw tears in Paul's eyes. The boy had been very anxious about his two friends, and now that he had Ranni's arm about him again, he was so relieved he felt almost like crying.

'Funny boy, isn't he!' whispered Mike to Jack. 'So

awfully brave, and yet he cries like a girl sometimes.'

'We'd better hide quickly,' said Ranni. 'The robbers may come back at any moment and we don't want them to find us all here. They would have five prisoners then, instead of two! Let's push the logs back exactly as they were, Mike. It will puzzle the robbers to know how we escaped, when they see that the logs have apparently not been moved!'

CHAPTER FOURTEEN

Back to the Robber Camp

IT WAS easy to shift the logs back into position for now Ranni and Pilescu were able to use the whole of their strength, instead of being hindered by being in a deep pit. They finished their task and then went to discuss their next move under some thick bushes at the edge of the clearing.

They had a good view of the path from there and could see anyone coming, though they themselves could not be seen. They sat down and talked earnestly. Jack told the two Baronians all that had happened, and they were amazed.

'Shall we try and get back home the way we came?' asked Mike. 'Perhaps that would be best.'

'I don't know about that,' said Ranni. 'Once the robbers discover that we are gone, they will be on the look-out for us, and probably men will be guarding the way back, ready to take us again.'

'Well, what else is there to do?' asked Paul, impatiently.

'Let us think carefully, little lord,' said Ranni. 'Can

there be any other way out of this Secret Forest, so well-hidden within the great Killimooin mountains?'

Everyone was silent. It was quite impossible to climb the surrounding mountains, even if they could make their way through the depths of the forest towards them.

Jack spoke at last. 'Ranni, where do you suppose this river goes to? It must go somewhere. If it was penned up in this valley, it would make a simply enormous lake, and it doesn't do that, or we should have seen it from the air, when we flew over.'

Ranni sat and thought. 'It must go somewhere, of course,' he said. 'Maybe it finds its way underground, as it did in the mountain. You think perhaps it would be a good idea to follow the river, Jack, and see if we can float away on it, maybe through a tunnel in one of the mountains, to the other side.'

'We could try,' said Jack, doubtfully. 'We could go back to the weird beehive-like houses tonight and see if our raft is still there. If it is, we could board it and go off on the river. The river won't take us backwards, that is certain, so we shall have to go forwards with it!'

'Well, we will try that,' said Ranni, though he did not sound very hopeful. 'Let us eat now, shall we? You must, as you said, be very hungry.'

The Baronians had brought the bread with them from

the pit. All five began to eat, thinking of the adventure that lay ahead. Pilescu looked at the three boys. He saw that they were worn out.

'We will find a good hiding place and rest there,' he said to Ranni. 'We shall need to be fresh for tonight. Come, then. I will carry Paul. He is already half asleep!'

But before they could creep away, they heard the sound of voices, and saw three or four robber-women coming down the path, carrying pitchers of water and more bread! They had evidently come to bring food to the prisoners. Very silently the five vanished into the trees.

The women went to the pit and placed the food and water beside it. They had apparently been told to take it there and leave it, so that the men could hand it down to the prisoners when they came later, and could move the logs a little apart. It was beyond the women's strength to move them.

The women peered curiously between the logs, and were amazed when they could not see the prisoners. They chattered together excitedly and then peered down again. It was dark in the pit, but even so, they should have been able to catch sight of the two men. Had not the children been to see them that morning and come back with tales of their fierce shouts and cries, their fiery red hair and beards? Then why could not these things be seen and heard now?

The women became certain that the prisoners were not there. Yet how could they have escaped? The logs were still across the mouth of the pit, and no men could move those without help from outside! It was a mystery to them. Chattering loudly, they fled away back to the robber encampment to tell the news. They left the food and water beside the empty pit.

As soon as the women had gone, Ranni slipped out of his hiding place and went to the pit. He took the bread and ran back to the others.

'This may be useful!' he said. He tied a leather thong around it, and hung it at his back. It was a flat, round loaf, easy to carry.

'Now we will find a good hiding place,' said the big Baronian. Pilescu picked up Paul in his arms and the two men strode away into the forest to find a safe hiding place to rest until night came.

Presently they found one. A great rock jutted up between the thickly growing trees, and underneath it was a well-hidden hole, draped by greenery. Once in the shelter of that rock, no one would see them.

'Do you know the way back to the clearing, Pilescu?' asked Paul, sleepily, as the big man arranged him comfortably on the ground, on the fur-lined cloaks that he and Ranni had taken off for the time being.

They made good rugs for the three tired boys.

'I know it, little lord. Do not worry your head,' said Pilescu. 'Now sleep. You must be wide-awake tonight, for you may need all your wits about you!'

The boys soon slept. They had had so little sleep the night before, and were so exhausted with all their adventures, that it was impossible to keep awake. The men kept a watch. They had been very touched to know that the boys had followed them to rescue them. Now it was their turn to watch over the boys, and save them from the robbers!

The sun began to slide down towards the west. The day was going. Ranni dozed, and Pilescu kept watch. Then Pilescu dozed whilst Ranni kept eyes and ears open. He heard excited cries towards the evening, coming from the clearing, and guessed that the robbers had discovered their escape. Then all was silence again. The Secret Forest was the most silent place that Ranni had ever been in. He wondered if the wind ever blew down in that valley, and if birds ever sang. It made him jump when a mouse-like creature scurried over his foot.

Twilight came creeping into the forest. It was always dim there, and difficult to see the sunshine. Twilight came there before the outer world had lost its daylight. Ranni looked at his watch. Half-past seven. The boys still slept.

Let them sleep for another hour or two, and then they would creep through the darkness of the forest, back to the clearing where they had left the raft.

Jack awoke first. He stretched himself and opened his eyes, looking into complete darkness. He wondered where he was. Then he heard Ranni speaking in a low voice to Pilescu, and everything came back to him. He was in the Secret Forest, of course – hidden under that rock! He sat up at once.

'Ranni! Pilescu! What time is it? Is everything all right?'

'Yes,' said Ranni. 'Soon we will go to get the raft. We will wake the others now, and eat. Paul! Mike! It is time to wake!'

Soon all five of them were eating the hard bread. Ranni had some water in his flask, and everyone drank a little. Then they were ready to go.

By the light of his torch Ranni made his way back to the clearing where the pit was. He flashed his light around. There was no one there at all. The logs had been dragged away from the pit, when the robbers had come to see if what their women had said was true.

'We will take the path back,' said Ranni. 'It is over there. Take hands and go in single file. We must not lose hold of one another. I go first. You next, Paul. Then Mike and Jack, and Pilescu last. Now – are you ready?'

They found the path and went along it quietly in single file. The boys felt excited, but perfectly safe now that they had Ranni and Pilescu.

Ranni halted after a while. He flashed his torch here and there. He had gone from the path!

'We are not very far from it,' he said. 'I saw the axe marks in a tree only a little way back. We must look for them.'

It was anxious work looking for the axe marks which would tell them they were once more on the right path. Mike felt very uncomfortable as he wondered what would happen if they really got lost in that enormous forest! He thought he saw two gleaming eyes looking at him from between the trees and he jumped.

'Is that a wolf?' he whispered to Jack. But it was only his imagination! There was no wolf, merely a couple of shining leaves caught in the light of Ranni's brilliant torch!

'Ah!' said Ranni, at last, in a glad voice. 'Here is the path again. And look, there are axe marks on that tree. Now we can go forward again. Keep a lookout, all of you, for the axe marks that tell us we are on the right path.'

Everyone watched anxiously for the marks after that. It was impossible to stray far from the path if they followed the marks. They were made at regular intervals, and the little company soon made steady progress.

'We must be near the encampment!' said Ranni at last, in a low voice. 'Can you hear the lapping of water? I think we are nearing that big pool.'

In another minute his torch shone on to the glittering waters of the pool. They had reached the cluster of huts. If only the robbers did not see or hear them!

CHAPTER FIFTEEN

A Way of Escape?

EVERYTHING WAS quiet. There were only a few small night sounds – the lapping of the water, the squeal of some small animal, the splash of a fish jumping. There was nothing else to be heard at all.

The five stood quite still beside the big pool, listening. A curious sound came on the air, and the boys clutched one another.

'It's all right,' whispered Ranni, a laugh in his voice. It's only one of the robbers snoring in the nearest hut!'

So it was. The sound came again, and then died away. Ranni, who had switched off his torch, switched it on again. He wanted to find the raft that Paul had told him about. Luckily it was quite near him, about ten yards away, tied to a tree.

'Did you come down the mountain river on a raft like that?' whispered Paul to Ranni. The big man answered in a low voice.

'We came on a raft only as far as the outlet of the river, just where it leaves the mountain. The men steered the raft to the bank there, and we all jumped off. They tied up the raft and we walked the rest of the way to the Secret Forest. Apparently, whenever the robbers go up to the temple cave they walk along the ledge beside the mountain river, and drag a raft up with them, floating it on the rushing water. It must be hard work!'

'Oh! Then that's why there are no rafts to be seen on this pool,' said Jack, who had been puzzling about this. 'They only use them inside the mountain, to bring them down quickly.'

'Sh!' said Pilescu, warningly. 'We had better not talk any more. Hold your torch higher, Ranni, so that I can see to untie the raft.'

It did not take long to free the raft. Ranni found a broken branch to use as a paddle. He did not want to be completely at the mercy of the river. With the branch to use, he could steer a little, and, if necessary, bring the raft to the bank.

'Get on the raft,' whispered Ranni. They all got into the hollowed-out piece in the centre, it was a tight fit! Ranni pushed the raft into the centre of the big pool, where it was caught in the current that flowed through it. The raft swung along at once, very slowly but surely. Soon it was out of the pool and on the river, which ran through the Secret Forest for miles.

It was very weird and mysterious, swinging along

on the swift river, through the heart of the dark forest. Sometimes branches of trees swept down low and bumped the heads of the travellers, scraping their faces. It was impossible to prevent them. Ranni tried shining his torch so that they might have warning of overhanging boughs but the river was swift, and the downsweeping branches were on them before they knew.

The boys huddled against one another, stiff and uncomfortable. When a big branch nearly took Paul overboard and gave him a great bruise on his forehead, Ranni decided to moor the raft till the night was over. He did not expect the robbers to pursue them down the river, because they had no boats.

So he tied the raft to a tree, and the five of them nibbled bread and talked in low voices. Ranni fell off to sleep after a while, but the boys were wide awake now. Pilescu kept watch. It seemed a long long time till dawn, but at last it came. The trees were so thick just there that the boys could see no sunlight, only a gradual lightening around them, as the tree trunks began to show, and the leaves to take on colour.

'We'll go on now,' said Ranni. He untied the raft and on they went again, caught by the strong current. Now they could see when branches of trees would scrape over the raft, and Ranni steered to avoid them.

The river wound in and out, and suddenly took a great curve, almost doubling back on itself.

'I hope it doesn't flow back very far!' said Pilescu. 'We don't want to land back near the robber camp!'

The river did wind back a good way, and at one part, although the little company did not know it, it was only about a mile from the robbers! It had a strange course in the Secret Forest. It flowed halfway through, doubled back, and finally flowed out of the trees about six miles from where it first flowed in. The travellers did not know this, though Ranni could tell, by the position of the sun, that they were now travelling almost in the opposite direction.

The trees suddenly thinned, and sunshine flooded down here and there, almost dazzling the two men and the three boys. The river flowed more rapidly, and the raft bobbed about.

'We are coming out of the Secret Forest!' said Jack, shading his eyes and looking forward. 'The trees are getting thinner and thinner. Where does this river go, I wonder? I do wish it would take us right through the mountains somewhere and out at the other side. Then we could just walk round them till we come to Killimooin Castle.'

'Not so easily done!' said Pilescu.

A shout made them turn their heads. To their horror,

between the trees, they saw one of the robbers! He called out something, and then ran off to tell his comrades, his red wolf-tail swinging behind him.

Six or seven more came running with him after a few minutes, and they stood watching the raft as it swung along in the distance.

One robber yelled something after them. 'What did he say?' asked Jack. Ranni looked a little solemn.

'He speaks a curious dialect,' he said, 'but I think I understood him to say, "Soon, soon, you will be in the middle of the earth!" I wonder what he meant?'

Everyone thought about it. 'Do you think it means that the river goes down underground?' asked Jack. 'Well if it does, it's what we want, isn't it?'

'It depends on whether there is room for the raft or not,' said Ranni. 'We must keep a sharp look-out.'

The river ran on. The boys saw the mountains of Killimooin around them. In front of them, slightly to the left, was the one they knew, on the other side of which Killimooin Castle was built. It looked very different from this side, but the summit was the same shape.

Suddenly they heard a terrific roaring sound ahead of them. Quick as thought Ranni plunged the tree-branch into the water and tried to steer the raft out of the current. But it was very swift and the raft kept on its course.

Jack saw that the big Baronian looked pale and anxious as he tried in vain to swing the raft from its steady course. 'What's the matter?' he asked.

'Can you hear that noise?' said Ranni. 'I think the river makes a fall somewhere ahead – maybe a big waterfall. We don't want to be caught in it. I can't get this raft out of the current.'

Pilescu suddenly slipped overboard, and, taking the raft with one hand, tried to swim to the shore with it. But he could not move it from the swift current.

'Jump!' he cried to the others. 'Jump, and swim. It is our only hope. We are getting near the fall.'

Everyone jumped into the water. Paul was the weakest swimmer and big Ranni took him on his back. The raft went bobbing off by itself.

Pilescu helped Mike and Jack, but it was a stiff struggle to get to the bank of the swiftly running river. They sat there, exhausted, hoping that no robber would come by, for they had no strength to resist anyone!

They recovered after a while. The hot sun dried their clothes, and steam began to rise from them.

'I wonder what happened to the raft,' said Jack.

'We'll go and see!' said Ranni. The noise is so tremendous here that the waterfall, or whatever it is, can't be very far ahead. I think it must be where that fine mist hangs in the air over there, like smoke.'

They walked on beside the river, over rough ground. The noise became louder and louder. Then they suddenly saw what happened to the mountain river!

They rounded a big rock and came to the place where fine spray flew. The great silver river rushed by them – and then disappeared completely!

No river flowed ahead. The whole of the water vanished somewhere in that little place. Ranni went forward cautiously. He called to the others:

'It's a good thing we got off the raft when we did! The river goes right down into the earth here!'

All the others joined Ranni. The spray soaked them as they stood there, trying to see where the volume of water went to.

It really was most extraordinary. There appeared to be a great cavern or chasm in the ground into which the river emptied itself with a terrific roar. The water fell into the enormous hole and completely disappeared.

'So that's what the robber meant when he shouted that we should soon be in the middle of the earth,' said Jack. 'That water must go deep down into enormous holes and crevices among the rocks. I suppose it goes right under the surrounding mountains and comes out somewhere else as a river again. How amazing!'

'What a mercy we leapt off the raft!' said Mike, feeling scared at the thought of what might have happened if they and the raft together had plunged down into the heart of the earth. 'Golly! This river has an exciting course! Through the mountain, down the slope, into the Secret Forest, out again, and down this chasm. Well – there's no way out for us here, that's certain.'

The five travellers left the curious place, and went to sit by a sun-warmed rock to dry their spray-wet clothes once more.

'The robbers must think we are all lost in the depths of the earth now,' said Pilescu. 'They will not be on the watch for us any more. That is something to the good, at any rate.'

'What are we going to do?' asked Paul.

'There is only one thing to do, my little lord,' said Pilescu. 'We must go back the way we came!'

'What! Up into the mountain, beside the river all the way, and back to the temple-cave?' cried Paul. 'Oh, we shall never do that!'

'We must,' said Ranni. 'It is the only way out. I am going to climb a high tree so that I may see where the river flows out of the mountain.'

He climbed up the biggest tree nearby, and shaded his eyes for a long time. Then he came down.

'I cannot see where the river comes forth from Killimooin,' he said. 'It is too far away. But I can see where the water enters the Secret Forest – or I think I can. We must go to the east, and walk until we come to the river. We cannot miss it, for it will lie right across our path!'

'Let us have something to eat first,' said Paul. 'Where is the bread? There is plenty left, isn't there?'

There was not plenty, but there was enough. They sat and ate hungrily. Then Ranni rose, and everyone got up too.

'Now to find the river again,' said Ranni. 'We will skirt the Secret Forest until we come to the rushing water. Then we will follow it upwards to the mountain!'

CHAPTER SIXTEEN

The Terrible Storm

MEANWHILE, WHAT had happened to the two girls? They had done as the boys had suggested, and had awakened Tooku and Yamen at once. The couple sat up in their bed, bewildered at the children's extraordinary story. Ranni and Pilescu captured by the robbers! The statue that split into two! All the boys gone! It seemed like an unbelievable nightmare to Yamen and Tooku.

'We can do nothing tonight,' said Tooku, nursing his injured arm. 'The servants would be of no use to hunt for the boys and the others. They would be too afraid. Tomorrow, early, we must send the servants to gather together the villagers of the mountainside.'

The girls did not want to wait so long, but there was nothing else to be done. They went back to bed, but not to sleep. They cuddled together on a small couch, covered with a warm fur rug, and talked together, worried about the boys. At last, just before dawn, they dozed off, and were awakened by Yamen.

Soon everyone in the castle knew what had happened

the night before. The servants went about with scared faces. Paul's mother heard the girls' story again and again, tears in her eyes as she thought of how Paul had marched off to rescue his men.

'He is a true little Baronian!' she said. 'How glad I am that Mike and Jack are with him! Oh, why didn't they wait until we could send soldiers or armed villagers to find Ranni and Pilescu?'

A band of people came climbing up on mountain ponies, fetched by servants of the castle and by the goatherd, Beowald. They had been amazed at the tale told to them, but all of them were determined to rescue their 'little lord' as they called Paul.

Beowald was with them. He led them up the hill to the old temple-cave. The villagers shrank back in fear when they saw the strange stone images. The statue of the sitting man, at the back, was now whole again. The robbers that the boys had seen the night before had come up to the cave, found the statue in half, and, fearing that their secret had been discovered, had closed the two halves together once more and gone back into the cave below.

Peggy and Nora watched Blind Beowald put his finger into the right ear of the statue. The villagers cried out in wonder when they saw the stone man split in half, and divide slowly. Beowald pointed down to the hole that the statue hid so well.

'That is the way,' he said.

The villagers went to the hole and looked down. They shivered. They did not want to go down at all. Thoughts of mysterious magic, of mountain spirits, filled their heads.

But one bolder than the rest slid down the rope, calling to the others to follow. One by one they went down. The girls wanted to go too, but Tooku and Yamen forbade them sternly. 'This is men's work,' they said. 'You would only get in the way.' So the girls had to go back to the castle, where Paul's mother sat waiting for news, white and anxious.

Nora and Peggy tried to comfort her by telling her of the adventures they and the boys had had before, and how they had always won through in the end. The Queen smiled at them, and sighed.

'You are adventurous children!' she said. 'Wherever you go, you have adventures. I shall be glad when this adventure is over!'

There was no news at all that day. The search party did not return. Beowald came down from the temple to say that although he had listened well by the hole, he had heard nothing. For the first time he was angry with his blindness, for he badly wanted to follow his friends into the mountain. But he did not dare to, because he would be completely lost in a place he did not know.

Towards teatime the sky suddenly darkened. The girls went to the window. Yamen was with them, and she looked out too.

'A storm is coming,' she said, pointing to the west. 'A great storm. You must not be frightened, little ones. Sometimes, when the weather has been hot, the big clouds blow up, and the lightning tears the sky in two, whilst the thunder roars and echoes round.'

'We are not afraid of storms, Yamen,' said Nora. 'It ought to be a wonderful sight, a storm in the Killimooin mountains!'

The sky grew so black that the girls could not see to read. Great clouds began to roll round the mountain itself, and soon the castle was completely swallowed up in the thick, swirling mists. Thunder rumbled in the distance. The little children in the nurseries of the castle began to cry.

'There's the lightning!' said Nora, as a vivid flash appeared, and everything was lighted up clearly for an instant. 'Oh – what thunder! I've never heard anything like it!'

Killimooin seemed to be in the midst of the storm.

Thunder cracked round the castle, and the lightning shivered the sky to pieces. It was as dark as night between the flashes.

Although the two girls were not afraid of storms, they were awed by this one. The noise was so terrific and the lightning was so grand.

Then the rain came. Rain? It sounded more like a waterfall pouring down on the castle, lashing against the windows, forming itself into rivulets that rushed down the hillside at top speed. Never in their lives had the two girls seen or heard such rain. It almost drowned the thunder that still rolled around!

'Well, it's a mercy the boys are not out in this, but are somewhere in a cave,' said Nora, trying to be cheerful.

But the boys were not in a cave! No, they were making their way towards the river where it entered the Secret Forest! They were almost there, and could see its shining waters. They were glad, because now they felt that they knew their way. They had only to follow the river's course backwards to the mountain, and climb up beside it as it flowed down through the heart of the hill!

Then the sky darkened, and the storm blew up. First, it was very still, and Ranni glanced uneasily at the sky. He knew the Baronian storms! They were as grand as the mountains themselves!

THE TERRIBLE STORM

The storm broke, just as the little party reached the river and began to follow its swift course backwards to the mountain. Thunder cracked above their heads, and lightning split the darkened sky.

'We had better shelter,' said Ranni, and looked about for somewhere to go. He did not want to stand under the trees in case they were struck by lightning. There were some thickly growing bushes nearby with enormous flat leaves. The rain fell off the leaves as if they were umbrellas.

'We'll crawl under these bushes,' said Ranni. 'We can draw our cloaks over our heads. The rain will not soak through the fur lining.'

But it did! It soaked through everything, and once again the company were wet! The boys hated the fierceness of this rainstorm. The drops pelted down, stinging them, slashing them, soaking through the bushes, their fur-lined cloaks, their clothes, and everything.

'What a storm!' said Paul. 'It is the worst I ever remember in Baronia. I don't like it, Pilescu.'

Pilescu pulled the small boy to him and covered him with his great arms. 'You are safe with Pilescu,' he said. 'Not even the worst storm can harm you now!'

For two hours the rain poured down, never ending. Jack was astonished to think that so much water could be held by clouds! It was as if someone up in the sky was emptying whole seas of water down on to the earth.

At last a break came in the clouds and a bit of brilliant blue sky showed through. The thunder died away. The lightning no longer flashed. The clouds thinned rapidly, and the rain stopped. The boys heaved sighs of relief. They were wet, cold and hungry. Ranni felt about in his big pockets and brought out some chocolate. It was very welcome.

'Now we must get on,' he said. 'If the sun comes out strongly, before it sets, we shall soon be dry again. We have a long climb ahead before we reach the place where the river gushes forth from the mountain. Shall I carry you for a while, little lord?'

'Certainly not,' said Paul. 'I can walk as well as Mike and Jack!'

But after three hours of hard walking the little prince was only too glad to be hoisted on to Pilescu's broad back! They made their way slowly on and up, the noise of the water always in their ears. They saw no sign of the robbers at all, though they kept a sharp look-out for them.

When evening began to fall they reached the place where the river flowed out of the mountainside, rushing and roaring as if in pleasure to see the sun. They sat by the water and rested. They were all tired now.

'Well, we must begin our watery climb now,' said Ranni, at last. 'It will take us some hours to follow the river up to where it falls into the cave above. The way will be steep and often dangerous. Paul, I am going to tie you to me, for if you fall into the river, I cannot save you. You will be whirled away from me in an instant.'

'Well, tie Mike and Jack to Pilescu, then,' said Paul. 'I don't want to be the only one.'

In the end, all five were roped together, so that if one fell, the others might pull him up again to safety. Then the five of them entered the cavernous hole in Killimooin mountain, and prepared to climb up beside the rushing torrent.

There was a narrow ledge, as Ranni had guessed. It was wet and slippery, and sometimes so narrow that it seemed impossible to walk on it. But by finding firm hand-holds in the rocky wall of the tunnel, the climbers managed to make their way steadily upwards.

Once Paul slipped and fell. He almost jerked Ranni off his feet, too. The boy half fell into the rushing water, but Ranni caught hold of the rope and tightened it quickly. The boy was pulled back to the ledge, and knelt there, gasping with fright.

'You are safe, little Paul. Do not be afraid,' said Ranni, comfortingly, shouting above the rushing of the water.

'I'm not afraid!' yelled Paul, and got to his feet at once. He had had a bad scare, but he would not show it. Ranni felt proud of the little prince.

They toiled upwards, not saying a word, because it was soon too much effort to shout to make themselves heard above the noise of the river. It seemed as if they had been climbing up the narrow ledge for hours, with Ranni's torch showing the way at the front, and Pilescu's at the back, when the five saw something that startled them exceedingly.

The light from Ranni's torch fell on something swirling down the torrent! In surprise Ranni kept his torch pointed towards it – and the little company saw that it was a raft, on which were five or six of the small, wiry robbers, bobbing rapidly downwards to the Secret Forest!

The robbers saw them too, and uttered loud cries of amazement. In half a minute they were swept away down the river, out of sight, lost in the long black tunnel through which the water rushed downwards.

'They saw us!' yelled Jack. 'Does it matter, do you think? Will they come after us?'

Ranni and Pilescu stopped to consider the matter. They thought it was possible that the robbers *would* turn back and pursue them. It would be easy to swing their raft against the side and leap out. They could drag their raft up behind them, as they apparently did each time they climbed up to the temple-cave.

'Ranni!' yelled Jack, again. 'Do you think they'll come after us?'

'We think it is likely,' replied Ranni. 'We must push on quickly. Come, there is no time to be lost.'

The five of them set off again. It was a hard and tiring journey. They were splashed continually by the river, which also overflowed time and again on to the ledge so that their legs were always wet. Sometimes the tunnel was very low, and once the company had to go down on hands and knees and crawl like that round a bend of the ledge, their heads touching the roof of the tunnel!

Ranni's torch gave out and Mike was glad he had one with him to lend to Ranni, for it was necessary to have two, one at the back of the line and one at the front.

'How much further have we to go?' groaned Paul. 'How much further, Ranni?'

CHAPTER SEVENTEEN

A Journey up the Mountain River

IT WAS a long, long climb. Ranni shone his torch on to his watch, and saw that it was nearly midnight! No wonder poor Paul was groaning, and wondering how much further they had to go. Even the two men were tired.

'Ranni, there's a sort of platform place somewhere,' said Jack, remembering the broadening out of the ledge, where he and the others had slept in a recess at the back two nights before.

Ranni and Pilescu did not know about this. Jack shouted into their ears, telling them about it, and the two Baronians hoped that they would soon come to it. Then they would all have a rest. One or other could be on watch in case the robbers came!

Up they went again, stumbling over the rough, rocky ledge that ran beside the river. Once Mike slipped and fell headlong into the water. He pulled Jack right off his feet, and both boys disappeared. Paul gave a scream of fright.

But Pilescu stood steady, and gripped the rope. He

pulled Jack and Mike firmly back to the side and helped the soaking boys out. They were shivering as much with fright as with cold! It was not at all a nice feeling to take a plunge unexpectedly into the icy mountain water. They were glad that Ranni had had the idea of roping everyone together. Jack hoped that neither of the big Baronians would fall into the river, for he was sure that if they did they would jerk the boys in after them! But Ranni and Pilescu were surefooted, having been used to climbing hills and mountains all their lives, and neither of them slipped!

Paul was getting so tired that he could hardly stumble along. It was impossible for Ranni to carry him, for he needed both his hands, one to hold the torch, and the other to find handholds for himself. His heart ached for the tired boy stumbling along just behind him.

It was a long time before they came to the platform. Ranni did not even know he had come to it. He went along the ledge, feeling the wall, not noticing at first that he was getting further from the river. Mike gave a shout.

'I believe it's the platform! Oh good! This ledge is widening out tremendously!'

Ranni and Pilescu stopped and flashed their torches around. It *was* the platform, as the boys called it! Thank goodness for that.

'There's the recess where we slept, look!' shouted Mike. The men saw the hollowed-out recess in the wall at the back, lined with fur rugs. They saw something else, too. On the little shelf above was more bread, placed there by the robbers the company had seen swinging down on their raft two or three hours before!

'Now this is really good,' said Ranni. He set Paul on his knee, took the bread, and broke it into pieces. Mike and Jack took some and began to eat hungrily. But Paul was too exhausted. He could eat nothing. His head fell forward on Ranni's broad chest, and he was asleep at once.

'You boys must rest on those rugs on that rocky couch there,' said Ranni, speaking to Mike and Jack. 'I will hold Paul in my arms to warm him. Pilescu will keep watch for the robbers in case they come back.'

Mike and Jack flung themselves on to the strange resting place at the back of the platform, and pulled the fur rugs over them. They were asleep in half a second. The two Baronians were sleepy too, but Pilescu was on guard and did not dare even to close his eyes.

Ranni fell asleep holding Paul. Only big Pilescu was awake. He felt his eyes closing. He had switched off his torch, for he did not want the robbers to see any light, if they came back. It was difficult to keep awake in the dark, when he was so tired!

His head nodded. He stood up at once. He knew it would be impossible not to sleep if he remained seated. He began to walk up and down the platform, like a lion in a cage. That kept him awake. He was not likely to fall asleep on his feet.

He paced steadily for two hours. Then he stiffened and listened. He could hear voices! They echoed up from the tunnel below. It must be the returning robbers!

'They have managed to get their raft to the side and land, and have turned back to come after us!' thought Pilescu. 'What are we to do? They will be on us before we can escape. How I wish I had a gun with me!'

But the robbers had taken away all the weapons carried by the Baronians. Neither Ranni nor Pilescu had anything to defend themselves with, except their bare hands. Well, they could make good use of those!

The voices came nearer. Pilescu woke Ranni and whispered the news to him. Ranni put the sleeping Paul into the recess at the back, with the other boys. He did not wake.

'We will cover ourselves with our cloaks and sit with our backs to the wall, on either side of the recess,' whispered Ranni. 'It is just possible that the robbers may not see us, and may not guess that we are resting here. They would think that we were going ahead as fast as we could.'

They could not hear any voices now. They guessed that the robbers were very near. They carried no torch but were coming along the ledge they knew so well, in complete darkness.

Ranni's sharp ears caught the sound of panting. A robber was on the platform! The two Baronians sat perfectly still, hoping that the three sleeping boys would make no sound. They had covered them completely with the rugs so that any snoring might not be heard. It was amazing that Ranni had been able to hear the robbers, because the river made almost as much noise there as anywhere else.

There came the sound of a loud voice and it was clear that all the robbers were now on the platform. Ranni and Pilescu strained their ears for any signs that the wolf-tailed men were going to explore the wide ledge.

There appeared to be no more sounds at all. Neither Ranni nor Pilescu could hear panting or voices. They sat like statues, hardly breathing, trying to hear any unusual sound above the noise of the water.

They sat like that for ten minutes without hearing a sound. Then, very silently, Ranni rose to his feet. He felt for his torch, and pressed down the switch suddenly. The light flashed out over the platform. It was quite empty!

'They've gone,' whispered Ranni. 'I thought they must

have, for I have heard nothing for the last ten minutes. They did not think of searching this platform. They have gone higher up, probably hoping to catch us in the cave where the great waterfall is.'

'That's not so good,' said Pilescu, switching off his torch. 'If they wait for us there, they will catch us easily. Jack said that Beowald was going to fetch the villagers to hurry after us – it is possible that they might have got as far as the waterfall cave, and might help us. But we can depend on nothing!'

'We will let the boys rest a little longer,' said Ranni. 'There is no need to rush on, now that the robbers are in front of us, and not at the back! I will watch now, Pilescu, whilst you sleep.'

Pilescu was thankful to be able to allow himself to close his eyes. He leaned his big head against the wall at the back, and fell into a deep sleep at once. Ranni was keeping guard, his eyes and ears on the look-out for anything unusual. It was a strange night for him, sitting quietly with his sleeping companions, hearing the racing of the mountain river, watching for wolf-tailed robbers to return!

But they did not return. There was no sound to make Ranni alert. The others slept peacefully, and the boys did not stir. Ranni glanced at his watch after a long time had passed. Six o'clock already! It was sunrise outside the mountain. The world would be flooded with light. Here it was as dark as midnight, and cold. Ranni was glad of his warm cloak.

Pilescu awoke a little while later. He spoke to Ranni.

'Have you heard anything, Ranni.

'Nothing,' said Ranni. 'It is nearly seven o'clock Pilescu. Shall we wake the boys and go on? There is no use in staying here. Even if the robbers are lying in wait for us above, we must push on!'

'Yes,' said Pilescu, yawning. 'I feel better now. I think I could tackle four or five of those ruffians at once. I will wake the boys.'

He awoke them all. They did not want to open their eyes! But at last they did, and soon sat munching some of the bread they had found on the little shelf nearby the night before.

Ranni told them how the robbers had gone by in the night without discovering them.

'It's not very nice to think they're somewhere further up, waiting for us!' said Mike, feeling uncomfortable. 'I suppose they'll be in one of the caves. We'll have to look out!'

'We'll look out all right!' said Jack, who, like Pilescu, felt all the better for his night's sleep. 'I'm not standing any nonsense from wolf-tailed robbers!'

They left the platform, and made their way to the ledge that ran beside the river, beyond the platform. As usual Ranni went first, having tied them all together firmly.

'It's not so very far up to the waterfall cave from here, as far as I remember,' said Jack. 'About two hours or so.'

They began to stumble along the rocky ledge again, the water splashing over their feet. The boys were surprised to find that the ledge was now ankle-deep in water.

'It wasn't when we came down this way,' said Mike. 'Was it as deep as this when you and Pilescu were brought down by the robbers, Ranni?'

'No,' said Ranni, puzzled. 'It barely ran over the ledge. Look out – it's quite deep here – the river is overflowing its channel by about a foot. We shall be up to our knees!'

So they were. It was very puzzling and rather disturbing. Why was the river swelling like that?

CHAPTER EIGHTEEN

In the Cave of the Waterfall

THE HIGHER they went, the deeper the water became that overflowed the ledge. The river roared more loudly, too. Ranni puzzled over it and then suddenly realised the reason.

'It is the terrific rainstorm that has caused the river to swell!' he called back, his voice rising over the roar of the water. 'The rain has soaked deep into the mountain, and has made its way to the river. You know what a rainstorm we had yesterday – it seemed as if whole seas of water had been emptied down on the earth. The river is swelling rapidly. I hope it doesn't swell much more, or we shall find it impossible to get along.'

This was a very frightening thought. It would be dreadful to be trapped in the mountain tunnel, with the rushing river rising higher and higher. The three boys put their best feet forward and went as quickly as they could.

When nearly two hours had gone by, they began to hope they were nearing the waterfall cave. The river by now had risen above their knees and it was difficult to stagger along, because the water pulled against them the whole time. Ranni and Pilescu began to feel very anxious.

But, quite suddenly, they heard the sound of the waterfall that fell down into the big cave! It could only be the waterfall they heard, for the noise was so tremendous. 'We are nearly there!' yelled Ranni.

'Look out for the robbers!' shouted back Jack.

They rounded the last bit of the ledge, and, by the light of Ranni's torch, saw that at last they were in the big cave, from which led the passage that would take them to the cave below the temple. They all felt very thankful indeed.

There was no sign of the robbers. The five of them went cautiously into the cave and looked round. By the light of Ranni's torch the waterfall seemed to be much bigger than they had remembered. It fell from a great hole in the roof of the cave, and then ran down the channel to the tunnel, where it disappeared.

'It is greater now,' said Ranni. 'It must be much swollen by all the rain that fell yesterday. It already fills the hole through which it falls.'

'What will happen if the hole can't take all the extra water?' asked Jack, curiously.

'I don't know,' said Ranni. 'Now, what shall we do next? Where are those robbers? Are they lying in wait for us somewhere? Are they up in the cave below the temple – or have they gone out on the mountainside to rob again?'

'Well there's nothing for it but to go and see,' said Pilescu. 'You boys stay down here, whilst Ranni and I go through the passage to the other cave.'

'No – we'll go with you,' said Paul, at once.

'That would be foolish,' said Pilescu. 'There is no need for all of us to put ourselves in danger. You will stay here until I or Ranni come back to tell you that it is safe for us all to go back down the mountainside to the castle.'

The boys watched the two big Baronians disappear into the narrow passage at the end of the cave opposite the great waterfall. It was difficult to stay behind and wait in patience. They sat in a corner and watched the tremendous fall of water at the other end of the cave.

'It's roaring as if it was angry!' said Jack. 'I don't believe that hole is big enough now for all the volume of water to pour through. It will burst it bigger. I'm sure of it!'

'Well, the hole's made through the solid rock,' said Mike. 'It will have to burst the rock!'

Even as they spoke, a frightening thing happened. The water falling from the roof seemed suddenly to become bigger in volume and noise – and the boys saw a great mass of rock fall slowly from the roof! As Jack had said, the hole was no longer big enough to take the rush of water, and the force of its rush had burst away part of the solid, rocky roof!

Water at once flowed over the floor of the cave, almost to the feet of the astonished boys. They leapt up at once, staring at the water falling from the roof at the other end of the cave.

'I say! I hope the whole roof doesn't give way!' said Jack. 'There must be a terrific rush of water to burst through the rock like that.'

Nothing more happened, except that the extra volume of water made more noise and flooded the floor of the cave almost up to where the boys stood.

'Well, anyway, we're safe,' said Mike. 'We are just at the opening of the passage that leads upwards to the other cave. The water comes from the other direction. If it gets deep in here we'll have to go up the passage, that's all, away from it.'

It got no deeper, however, so the boys waited patiently. Twenty minutes went by, and there was no sign of the return of Ranni or Pilescu. Mike began to feel worried.

'I wish they'd come back,' he said. 'I feel as if I can't stay here doing nothing much longer!'

'Whatever are Ranni and Pilescu doing?' said Jack, impatiently. 'They must be right out on the mountainside by now!'

'Let's go up the passage and find out,' said Paul, at last. 'I simply can't sit here any longer.'

'All right,' said Mike. 'Come on. We can easily rush back if we hear Ranni and Pilescu coming.'

They made their way up the narrow, curving passage, leaving behind them the noise of the great waterfall. But before they were halfway up, they heard the sound of someone else coming down!

'That must be Ranni and Pilescu coming back!' said Mike, in a low voice. 'Come on – we'll get back. We don't want to get into trouble for not waiting, as we were told.'

They stumbled back down the rocky passage, and came out once more into the cave of the waterfall. It was still falling at the other end, with a mightier roar than ever.

'Here they come!' said Mike, as a light shone out of the passage. He flashed his own torch upwards to welcome Ranni and Pilescu.

And then he and the other two boys stared in horror. Certainly it was Ranni and Pilescu returning – but returning as prisoners! Once again they were captives, angry, but completely helpless! Six or seven robbers were behind them, kicking them and pushing them on.

'Ranni! What's happened?' cried Paul, springing forward.

But before anything could be explained, the robbers, with cries of satisfaction, leapt at the three boys and forced their arms behind them. Mike tried his hardest to get out his scout-knife but it was impossible!

The robbers bound the boys' arms and legs together with thongs of supple leather. No matter how they struggled, they could not free themselves. They were placed on the floor of the cave, like trussed chickens. Ranni and Pilescu stood roaring like angry bulls, trying to free their own hands, which had been tightly tied behind them as before. The robbers tripped them deftly to the ground and tied their legs together, too.

Small as they were, the Secret Forest robbers were very strong. Ranni and Pilescu were big giants of men, but the robbers swarmed over them like ants, and by their very smallness and deftness they overcame the two big men.

The robbers chattered together exultantly. Now they had all five prisoners to take back. But suddenly one of them pointed to the water that flowed over the floor of the cave.

They all looked at it in surprise. Clearly they had never seen water flowing over the floor of the cave before. They looked at the water falling from the now bigger hole in the roof of the cave, at the other end. They saw what had happened, and ran fearfully to the ledge that ran beside the roaring river.

The water was now above their knees. They had left their raft behind them, below the platform ledge. They gazed in panic at the water. They could not hear themselves speak, so near the waterfall, and ran back to where the five prisoners were, shouting to one another in terror.

The noise of the water grew louder. Everyone gazed fearfully at the hole through which it poured from the roof. And then more of the rocky roof gave way and fell to the floor of the cave with a crash. Water followed it at once, forcing its way out, pouring down into the cave with a noise like thunder.

The robbers gave a scream of terror. They knew that never would they be able to get back to the Secret Forest if they did not go at once, for now that more and more water was pouring down, the river in the mountain tunnel would rise so high that no one would be able to walk beside it on the rocky ledge.

They disappeared in the spray. Jack raised his head and saw them dimly in the distance, trying to force their way on to the ledge beside the river where it entered the tunnel. It was above their waists!

'They'll all be drowned,' said Jack. 'The water will sweep them off the ledge. It's getting deeper and deeper.'

'Don't worry about the robbers!' said Ranni, sitting up with a jerk. 'It's ourselves we must worry about! Look at the water – it's right up to us now!'

So it was. It lapped round them. The five captives managed to get themselves upright, though it was difficult, with both hands and feet tied. They struggled with their bonds, but the robbers were too clever at knots for them to be undone or broken.

'We'd better try to get up the passage,' said Ranni, trying to hop towards it with his tied-up legs. But he fell at once. He cracked his head against a rock, for he could not save himself with his hands. He lay quite still, and Paul looked at him in terror.

'He's just knocked out for a minute or two, that's all,' said Pilescu, comfortingly. But really, the big Baronian was as frightened now as little Paul. They were all in a terrible plight. At any moment more of the roof might fall in and the cave would be completely flooded with water. They could not help themselves to escape because they were so tightly bound.

'Ranni! Open your eyes!' begged Paul. One of the robbers had left a torch shining on a ledge nearby, and its light shone on to Ranni's face, as he lay with his eyes shut, half-leaning against the rocky wall. Pilescu! How did you get caught like this?'

'We went up into the cave below the temple,' said Pilescu. 'We found the statue was divided into half, and we climbed up. We could not see a robber anywhere. We went to the mouth of the cave and looked out. We could see nothing at all, because there is a thick mist on the mountainside this morning. We went back into the cave to return to you, when into the cave rushed all the robbers and flung themselves on us. They must have seen us standing at the entrance. They were waiting for us there! We could not see them in the mist.'

'Oh, Pilescu – just as we had got to the end of our journey!' cried Prince Paul. 'What are we going to do now? Is Ranni badly hurt? He hit his head so hard on the rock!'

Ranni opened his eyes at that moment and groaned. His head ached badly. He tried to sit upright, and then remembered everything with a rush.

'More of the roof is falling!' cried Jack. He was right. With another tremendous roar a great mass of rock again fell down at the other end of the cave, and a still greater volume of water poured out. It was now all round their legs. The five captives struggled to get up on ledges out of the way of it.

'It is rising higher now,' said Mike, watching the water swirling in the cave. The bright light of the torch glittered on the blackness of the icy-cold water. It looked very threatening.

'Pilescu, what *are* we going to do?' said Jack, desperately. 'We shall all be drowned soon if we don't do something! Oh, why didn't someone come after us – some of the servants, or villagers. Beowald said he would fetch some!'

Beowald, of course, *had* fetched the villagers, and they had gone down as far as the cave of the waterfall. But they had not been able to guess that the way the boys had gone was along the narrow, rocky ledge beside the rushing river. They had left the cave and gone back to the mountainside, telling Beowald that he must be mistaken. No one had gone down into those caves below! The robbers and their prisoners must be somewhere on the mountainside!

They had searched the mountains well, helloing and shouting for hours. When the thick mist had come up, they had had to leave their search, for, good mountaineers as they were, they could lose themselves in the mist as easily as any child.

Beowald alone had not stopped searching. The mist did not hinder him, for neither darkness nor mists made any difference to him. He wandered about all night long, looking for his friends, the big mountain goat keeping him company.

When the sun was high in the sky Beowald made his way back to the temple-cave. He listened outside. There was no sound. He went to the big stone image at the back. It was still split in half. Beowald stood thinking. Should he go down himself, and seek for the others? The villagers had already said there was nothing below but empty caves, with rushing water in one. Beowald would be lost in a strange place. But something made him decide to try.

The blind goatherd slipped down into the hole, hanging deftly on to the rope. Down he went, and down, and came at last to the little cave below. He explored it carefully with his hands stretched out in front of him, going round the rocky, irregular walls.

He soon found the opening that led into the narrow, rocky passage. He went down it, feeling before him and beside him with his hands. Down and down went the passage, curving as it descended.

Beowald came out into the cave of the waterfall, and stood there, deafened by the roar. Water swirled over his feet. At first he was so deafened by the terrific noise that he heard nothing more.

And then, to his extreme astonishment, he heard his name called.

'Beowald! Beowald!'

'Look – it's Beowald! Beowald, help us, quickly!'

IN THE CAVE OF THE WATERFALL

Beowald the goatherd stood at the entrance of the waterfall cave, his blind eyes seeing nothing, his ears hearing voices he could hardly believe in!

But even more astonished were the five captives! Beowald had appeared before them, like a wizard, just as they had given up all hope of being saved!

CHAPTER NINETEEN

Beowald to the Rescue!

'BEOWALD! QUICK! Set us free!' shouted Ranni. The water was already high, and more and more was flooding into the cave. It had increased a great deal in the last few minutes. Ranni was afraid that the whole roof might give way beneath the terrific weight of water – and then there would be no hope for the little company at all.

'What is it? Where are you? What is this water?' cried Beowald, lost in this strange new world of roaring and wetness.

'Beowald! Listen to me!' shouted Ranni, urgently. 'Listen carefully. You are standing at the entrance to a cave, where I and the others are, all bound tightly, so that we cannot walk, or free ourselves. Water is pouring into our cave, and we shall be drowned if you do not hurry. Step down, Beowald, walk towards my voice. Do not be afraid.'

'I will come,' said the blind goatherd. He stepped further into the water, and then stopped, afraid. He was never afraid in his own mountain world. He knew every inch, every rock, every tree. But this was all new to him and strange to him, and it frightened him.

'Hurry, Beowald, hurry!' cried Ranni. 'Come to me, quickly. Get out your knife. Cut my bonds.'

Beowald stumbled through the water and felt about for Ranni. His hands brushed the big Baronian's face. Ranni was half-lying, half-sitting. On his head was an enormous bump where he had struck it against a rock. Beowald's fingers felt the bump, and he wondered what had caused it. His hands ran down Ranni's body and he felt that the man had his arms tied behind his back.

He took out his knife and, with a careful stroke, cut the leather thongs that bound Ranni's hands together. The big man stretched out his arms gladly, trying to get some strength back into them for they were stiff and swollen with being bound so tightly.

He snatched Beowald's knife from him and cut the thongs that bound his ankles together. He stood up, and at once overbalanced, for the thongs had cut into his legs, and for the moment he could not stand on them. He rose again, and went to Paul.

In a trice the small boy was free, and was trying to get to the entrance of the passage. 'Quick, quick!' he cried. 'Set the others free, Ranni. They will be drowned!'

As quickly as he could Ranni cut the thongs that bound

the others, and set them free. They tried to stagger out of the water that now swirled above their knees. The cave was rapidly filling.

Ranni picked up the torch that was still lying on the rocky ledge, shining brightly into the cave. He held it so that everyone could see how to get into the narrow passage that led upwards to the other cave, away from the water. Beowald had already gone into the passage, anxious to get back to the mountainside he knew. He felt so strange and so lost underground.

Ranni swung his torch round the cave of the waterfall for the last time – and then he saw that what he had feared might happen, was about to happen! The whole roof of the big cave was giving way! The pressure and weight of the water above it, trying to find its way out of the already enlarged hole, was too much for it. It had to give way. The rain that had fallen in torrents on the mountaintop, had to get away somewhere, and it had found the ordinary channels in the mountain too small for it. It was forcing and pressing everything in its way – and now the roof of the cave had to give in to its enormous pressure.

With a terrific roar the roof fell in, and after it poured the biggest volume of water that Ranni had ever seen. He gave a shout of terror and rushed up the narrow passage after the others. He was afraid that the water might flood even that passage, and trap them before they could get into the other cave!

'What's the matter, Ranni, what's the matter?' cried Paul, hearing the terrified shout.

'Hurry! Hurry! The roof has fallen in and the cave is nothing but swirling water!' panted Ranni. 'It will find its way up this passage, before it can get its own level and drain away downwards. Hurry, Paul; hurry, Mike!'

The five in front of him, frightened by the fear in his voice, hurried on as swiftly as they could, stumbling over the rough, rocky way. Beowald was terrified. He was afraid of falling, afraid of the unknown, afraid of the roaring of the water behind him.

The water had found the narrow passage and was making its way up there too. Ranni felt sure he could hear it lapping behind him! He pushed the others on, shouting and yelling, and they, full of panic, went staggering through the dark and winding passage.

'Thank goodness the passage goes upwards all the way,' thought Ranni, thankfully, as he came to a steep piece. 'Now we are safe! The water cannot reach us here. We are too high. Never will anyone be able to get down into the cave of the waterfall again. There will always be water there now that the roof has fallen in.'

They came out into the cave below the temple at last.

All of them sank down on the floor, trembling in every limb. Surely there had never been such a narrow escape.

'If Beowald had not come when he did, we should all have been drowned by now,' said Paul, in a choking voice. 'Oh Beowald – however was it you came down there just at that moment?'

Far away, down the passage, the muffled roar of the water could still be heard. Beowald's voice rose clearly above it:

'The search party went down to this cave and to the waterfall cave, but they could not find you. They are seeking for you still out on the mountain. I was anxious, and when I came into the temple-cave, I felt that I must come down by myself, though I was afraid. That is how I found you.'

'We have had such adventures!' said Mike, beginning to feel quite a hero. 'We've been to the Secret Forest, Beowald!'

'That is marvellous,' said the blind goatherd. 'Surely no man has even set foot there before!'

'Oh, yes!' said Paul. 'The robbers live there, Beowald. They must have lived there for years and years. Ranni, will the robbers ever be able to come up the mountain river now, climbing along that ledge, to get to Killimooin this side?'

'Never,' said Ranni. 'We are well rid of them!'

Little by little the boys stopped trembling from their exertions, and their hearts beat less fast. They began to feel able to stand. Mike got up and found that he was quite all right again.

'I want to get back to the castle,' he said. 'I want to see the girls and tell them all that has happened to us. My word, won't they be jealous of our adventures!'

'I want something to eat,' said Paul. 'I'm terribly hungry. I shall ask Yamen to give me the very nicest, most delicious food she's got.'

The thought of food made everyone eager to set out again. Ranni got up and pulled Paul to his feet. 'Well, come along then,' he said. 'We shall soon be home now!'

One by one they hauled themselves up the rope that led to the temple-cave. Their feet found the rough places to help them, as they went up, and at last all six of them were standing in the big temple-cave.

It seemed dark there, darker than it should have been. Ranni looked towards the entrance.

'We can't go home!' he said in disappointment. 'Look at that mist! It is like a thick fog. We could not see our hands in front of our faces if we went out in that. We should be completely lost in two minutes.'

'Well, we must stay here till the mist clears,' said

Pilescu. 'I am afraid it will not clear for some hours. When the mountain mists are as thick as this one, they last a long time.'

'Oh, Pilescu! We *must* get back now we're so near home!' said Paul, almost in tears. 'We must! I'm so hungry I can't stay here one more minute.'

Jack looked at the blind goatherd, who was standing, quietly listening.

'Beowald can guide us back,' said Jack. 'You know your way by night, or in the thickest mist, don't you, Beowald?'

Beowald nodded. 'It is all the same to me,' he said. 'If you wish, I will take you back to Killimooin Castle. My feet know the way! Is the mist very thick? I can feel that there is one, but I do not know how thick.'

'It's the thickest one I've ever seen,' said Pilescu, peering out. 'I'm not at all sure I like to trust myself even to you, Beowald!'

'You are safe with me on the mountainside,' said the goatherd. He took out his little flute and played one of his strange tunes on it. An enormous horned head suddenly appeared at the entrance of the cave, and everyone jumped in fright.

'Ha, old one, you are there!' cried Beowald, as he heard the patter of the big goat's hooves. 'Keep by me, old one, and together we will lead these friends of ours safely down our mountainside!'

'Take hands,' ordered Ranni. 'Don't let go, whatever you do. If anything happens, and you have to let go, shout and keep on shouting so that we keep in touch with one another. We have had enough narrow escapes for one day!'

Everyone took hands. Beowald went out of the cave, playing his flute, his left hand firmly clasped in Ranni's big one. Behind Ranni came Paul, then Mike, then Jack, then Pilescu, all firmly holding hands.

'I feel as if we're going to play "Ring a ring of roses"!' said Jack, with a laugh.

'Well, don't let's play the "all-fall-down" part,' said Mike at once. 'It wouldn't be at all a good thing to do on a steep mountainside like this.'

They felt light-hearted at the idea of going home at last. With Beowald's music sounding plaintively through the mist, they stumbled along down the steep mountain path. Two or three times one or other of the boys fell, and broke hands. They shouted at once, and the party stopped and joined together again.

It was slow work walking in the thick mist. They could barely see the person in front. Only Beowald walked steadily and surely. He could see with his feet!

'Don't go too fast, Beowald,' said Ranni, as he felt the

little prince dragging behind him. 'Remember, we cannot see anything – not even our own feet.'

'Neither can Beowald!' thought Mike. 'How marvellous he is! Whatever should we have done without him?'

They stumbled downwards slowly for more than an hour and a half. Then Ranni gave a shout.

'We're almost there! I can hear the hens clucking at the back of the castle, and a dog barking. Bear up, Paul, we are nearly home!'

They came to the flight of steps, and stumbled up them, tired out. Beowald slipped away with the big goat. The others hardly saw him go. They were so excited at getting back safely. Killimooin Castle at last! They hammered on the big iron-studded door impatiently.

CHAPTER TWENTY

The End of the Adventure

THE DOOR flew open – and there stood Yamen with Nora and Peggy close behind her. With screams of excitement and delight the two girls flung themselves on the boys. Yamen beamed in joy. The lost ones were home again! They were dragged indoors, and Yamen ran up the big stone staircase, shouting at the top of her voice:

'Majesty! They're back! The little prince is safe! He is safe!'

The whole household gathered to hear the story of the returned wanderers. Servants peered round the door. The smaller children, clinging to the hands of their nurses, gazed open-eyed at the untidy, dirty boys and the two big Baronians. Tooku, his arm still bound up, came running up from the kitchen. What an excitement there was!

'We've been to the Secret Forest!' announced Paul, grandly. He had forgotten his tiredness and his hunger. He was the Prince of Baronia, back from rescuing his men.

'The Secret Forest!' repeated Yamen, with awe in her

voice, and all the servants sighed and nodded to one another. Truly their prince was a prince!

'No, Paul, no – you cannot have been there!' said his mother. She glanced at Ranni and Pilescu, who nodded, smiling.

'It's true, Mother,' said Paul. 'We found that Ranni and Pilescu had been captured by the robbers, and taken down below the temple-cave. There's a mountain river flowing underground there, and it's the only way there is to the Secret Forest!'

Bit by bit the whole story came out. Everyone listened, entranced.

When Paul came to the part where the roof had fallen in and they had almost been drowned, his mother caught him up into her arms, and wept tears over him. Paul was very indignant.

'Mother! Let me go! I'm not a baby, to be cried over!'

'No – you're a hero, little lord!' said Yamen, admiringly. 'I go to get you a meal fit for the greatest little prince that Baronia has ever had!'

She turned and went down to her kitchen, planning a really royal meal. Ah, that little Paul – what a prince he was! Yamen marvelled at him, and at the two English boys, as she quickly rolled out pastry on her kitchen table. She would give them such a meal. Never would they forget it!

THE END OF THE ADVENTURE

'Where is Beowald?' asked the Queen, when she had listened again and again to the thrilling tale of how Beowald had appeared just in time to free them before the cave filled with water. 'I must thank Beowald and reward him.'

'Didn't he come in with us?' said Jack. But no, Beowald was not there. He was far away on his mountainside, playing to his goats, hidden by the mist.

'Mother, I want Beowald to come and live with me,' said Paul. 'I like him, and he plays the flute beautifully. That shall be his reward, mother.'

'If he wants to, he shall,' promised the Queen, though she did not think that the blind goatherd would want such a reward. 'Now, you must get yourselves clean, and then a good meal will be ready. Oh, how thankful I am that you are all back in safety!'

Half an hour later the whole party looked quite different. They were clean again, and had on spotless clothes. How tired they looked, thought the girls. But perhaps they were only hungry!

Yamen had prepared a marvellous meal. The smell of cooking came up from the big kitchen, and the five travellers could hardly wait for the first dish to appear – a thick, delicious soup, almost a meal in itself!

The boys had never eaten so much before. Ranni and

Pilescu put away enormous quantities, too. Paul had to stop first. He put down his spoon with a sigh, leaving some of his pudding on his plate.

'I can't eat any more,' he said, and his eyelids began to close. Pilescu gathered him up in his arms to carry him to bed. Paul struggled feebly, half asleep.

Put me down, Pilescu! I don't want to be carried! How could you treat me like a weakling?'

'You are no weakling, little lord!' said Pilescu. 'Did you not rescue me and Ranni by your own strength and wisdom? You are a lion!'

Paul liked hearing all this. 'Oh, well, Mike and Jack are lions too,' he said, and gave an enormous yawn. He was asleep before he reached his bedroom, and Pilescu undressed him and laid him on the bed, fast asleep!

The girls hung on to Mike and Jack, asking questions and making them tell their story time and again.

'We were so worried about you!' said Nora. 'When the villagers came and said they couldn't find any of you, it was dreadful. And oh, that terrible storm! We hoped and hoped you were not caught in it.'

'Well, we were,' said Jack, remembering. 'And it was all because of that storm, and the torrents of rain that came with it, that the waterfall in the cave became so tremendous and swelled up the river that ran from it. I wonder if the robbers got down safely! My word, if they got down to where they left their raft, and got on to it, they'd go down that river at about sixty miles an hour!'

'Now Mike and Jack, you must go to bed, too,' said big Ranni, coming up. 'Paul is fast asleep. You have had a very hard time, and you need rest, too. Come.'

The children themselves could hardly believe that all their adventures really had happened, when they awoke next day. The boys lay and blinked at the ceiling. They felt stiff, but happy. They had rescued Ranni and Pilescu. They had found the robbers. They had been in the Secret Forest. They couldn't help feeling very pleased with themselves.

'Mother, I'm going up on the mountainside to find Beowald,' said Paul at breakfast time. 'I'm going to tell him he must leave his goats and come to live with me. When we go back to the palace he must come too. I shall never forget all he did for us.'

'Take Ranni and Pilescu with you,' said his mother. 'I'm afraid of those robbers still.'

'You needn't be,' said Paul. 'You will never see them again! Ranni! Will you come with me, and find Beowald!'

Ranni nodded. He and Pilescu looked none the worse for their adventure, except that Ranni had a great bump on his head.

The mist had entirely gone. The mountains shone clear all around, their summits sharp against the sky. The five children, with Ranni and Pilescu, mounted their ponies, and turned their shaggy heads up the mountainside.

They came to the temple-cave after about an hour. Beowald was not anywhere there. Ranni lifted his great voice and shouted down the mountainside:

'BEOWALD! BEOWALD!'

They heard an answering cry, musical and clear, coming from a distance. They sat down to wait for the blind goatherd. Paul was already planning a uniform for him. He would show Beowald what princely gratitude was!

Soon the children heard the playing of the little flute Beowald always carried with him. Then, rounding a curve nearby came a flock of capering goats. At the head of them marched the old goat with his big curling horns.

'Here he comes!' said the little prince, and he ran to meet the goatherd. Beowald came to sit down with the company, asking them how they felt after their adventure.

'Oh, Beowald – it was a thrilling time,' said Paul. 'I don't know what would have happened to us if it hadn't been for you. I want to reward you, Beowald. We are all grateful to you – but I, most of all.'

'Do not speak to me of rewards, little lord,' said the goatherd, and he played a little tune on his flute.

'Beowald, I want you to come and live with me,' said Paul. 'You shall come back to the big palace, and I will give you a uniform. You shall no longer herd goats on the mountainside! You shall be my man and my friend!'

Beowald looked towards the little prince with his dark, empty eyes. He shook his head and smiled.

'Would you make me unhappy, little prince? I would break my heart in a strange place, under a roof. The mountains are my home. They know me and I know them. They know the feel of my feet, and I know the song of their winds and streams. And my goats would miss me, especially this old one.'

The big horned goat had been standing by Beowald all the time, listening as if he understood every word. He stamped with his forefoot, and came close to the goatherd, as if to say, 'Master, I agree with you! You belong here! Do not go away!'

'I did so want to reward you,' said Paul disappointed.

'You *can* reward me, little lord,' said Beowald, smiling. 'Come to see me sometimes, and let me play my tunes to you. That will be enough reward for me. And I will make you a flute of your own, so that you too may learn the mountain songs and take them back to the big palace with you.'

'Oh, I'd like that,' said Paul, picturing himself at once

playing a flute, and making all the boys at school stare at him in admiration. 'You must teach me all the tunes you know, Beowald!'

'Let's go into the cave and have a look round,' said Jack. They all went in, but Ranni and Pilescu forbade the children to slip down the hole to the cave below.

'No,' he said. 'No more adventures whilst we are here! We have had enough to last us for a lifetime – or, at any rate, for two months!'

'Now the Secret Forest will never again be visited by anyone!' said Mike. 'The only way to it is gone. The water will always keep people from travelling through the mountain to get to it.'

'And the robber-people will never be able to leave the Secret Forest!' said Jack. 'How strange! They will have to live there, year after year, a people lost and forgotten.'

This was a strange thought. 'But perhaps it is a good punishment for robbers,' said Nora, thoughtfully. 'It will be like keeping them in a great prison, which they can never escape from to rob other people!'

'We shall never see the Secret Forest again,' said Mike, sadly. 'It is such an exciting place!'

But he was wrong. They did see it again, for when, towards the end of a lovely holiday, their mother and father flew over in the White Swallow to fetch the children,

THE END OF THE ADVENTURE

Ranni took the whole company, Captain and Mrs Arnold as well, in the blue and silver aeroplane, right over the Killimooin mountains, and over the Secret Forest!

'There it is, Daddy!' cried Mike. 'Look! You can see where the river flows out of the mountain. Go down lower, Ranni. Look, there's where it goes into the Secret Forest – and where it comes out again, after doubling back on itself. Oh, and there's where it disappears into a chasm, falling right down into the heart of the earth!'

The aeroplane was now so low that it almost seemed as if it was skimming the tops of the trees! The robbers heard the great noise, and some of them ran out from the forest in wonder.

'There's one of the robbers – and another – and another!' shouted Paul. 'Goodbye, robber-people! You'll have to live in the Secret Forest for ever and ever and ever.'

The aeroplane swept upwards and left the Secret Forest behind. Over Killimooin it went, and the children heaved a sigh.

'It's been the loveliest holiday we've ever had!' said Nora. 'I wonder what adventures we'll have *next* time?'

'You've had quite enough,' said Ranni.

But they are sure to have plenty more. They are that kind of children!

BONUS BLYTON!

Turn the page for exciting extras
by Enid Blyton to read and share!

Here are some illustrations from the first edition of *The Secret Forest*, published in 1943. The illustrations are by an artist named Eileen A. Soper, who illustrated many of Enid Blyton's books in the 1940s and 1950s.

THE CHILDREN COULD SEE THE COUNTRY BELOW, SPREAD OUT LIKE AN ENORMOUS, COLOURED MAP

'THERE'S AN EAGLE!' SAID NORA, SUDDENLY

THE GOATHERD WAS PLAYING HIS STRANGE,
UNENDING MELODIES

A BIG BRANCH NEARLY TOOK PAUL OVERBOARD

The Secret
of Moon Castle

*Here is the beginning of Enid Blyton's next Secret Stories
adventure,* The Secret of Moon Castle*!*

CHAPTER ONE

Home from School

TWO GIRLS were standing at their front gate one sunny
afternoon in July.

'The car ought to be here by now,' said Nora. 'I hope
it hasn't had a puncture or anything. I'm longing to see
Mike – and Jack too, of course.'

'So am I,' said Peggy, her sister. 'I wonder if Paul will
be with them? Is he going to spend his holidays with us –
or go back to Baronia? I wonder.'

Paul was the little Prince of Baronia, a great friend of
Nora, Peggy, Mike and Jack. He went to the same school
as the boys, and had had plenty of adventures with them.

'I expect he'll spend a few days with us first,' said Nora,
swinging on the gate. 'He usually does, doesn't he? Then
he'll have to go back to Baronia to see his parents – and all

his many brothers and sisters!'

'It's a silly idea, our school breaking up two whole days before the boys' school,' said Peggy. 'We go back earlier too – that's even more of a nuisance!'

'Here's a car – and it's bringing the boys!' said Nora, suddenly. 'They've come in Paul's car – the big blue and silver one. I wonder if Ranni is driving it?'

Ranni was Paul's man, who had vowed to look after Paul from the moment when he was put into his arms on the day he was born. He was devoted to the little prince, and had shared many adventures with him. And now here he was, driving the great Baronian blue and silver car, bringing the three boys home in state!

The girls swung the big gates open as the car came near. They yelled as the car swept in. 'Mike! Jack! Paul! Hurrah! Welcome back!'

The car stopped with a squeal of brakes, and Ranni, who was at the wheel, smiled at them through his fiery red beard. Three heads were poked out of the nearest window.

'Hello, girls! Jump in. We thought you'd be looking for us!' called Mike. The door was swung open, and the girls squeezed in at the back with the three boys making room for them.

Nora gave Mike a hug. He was her twin, and the two were very fond of each other. Except that Nora was smaller than Mike, they were very much alike, with black, curly hair and bright, merry eyes. Golden-haired Peggy was a year older, but Mike was as tall as she was.

'Hello!' said Jack, giving each of the girls a friendly punch. 'What do you mean by breaking up sooner than we did!'

Jack was not their brother. He had no parents, and the Arnolds had adopted him as a big brother for Mike, Nora and Peggy. He thought the world of them all, and grinned around happily, his blue eyes shining in his brown face.

Prince Paul never punched the girls in the friendly way that the other boys did. Baronian manners did not allow that! He bowed politely to each of the girls, smiling happily – but they hadn't the beautiful manners of Baronia, and fell on him like a couple of puppies.

'Is he still ticklish? Yes, he is! Paul, are you going to stay with us for the holidays – or just for a few days – or what?'

'Stop tickling me,' said Paul, trying to push them off. 'Hey, Ranni, Ranni! Stop the car and turn them out!'

The car swept up to the front door, and Ranni leapt out, grinning. He went to the back to get the school trunks piled there on top of one another.

The door flew open and Mrs Arnold stood there smiling. 'Welcome back, boys!' she said. Mike ran to hug his mother. 'We're home!' he shouted. 'Good old home!'

Jack kissed Mrs Arnold, and then Paul followed his usual custom, bent over her hand with a deep bow, and kissed it politely. The others used to laugh at Paul's grand manners, but they had got so used to them by now that they didn't really notice them.

'Come along in,' said Mrs Arnold. 'We'd better get out of Ranni's way. He's bringing the trunks in. Ranni, how can you manage two trunks at once?'

Ranni grinned. He was big, and enormously strong. Two trunks were nothing to him! He went up the stairs with them easily.

'Mother! What a lovely smell!' said Mike, sniffing. 'Buttered toast – and hot scones!'

'Quite right,' said his mother. 'You've probably forgotten that you asked me to have them for tea as soon as you got home these holidays – though why you took it into your head to ask for such things on a hot July day I don't know.'

Jack put his head in at the dining-room door. Tea was already laid there. 'Goodness!' he said. 'Home-made éclairs too – and the biggest chocolate sponge sandwich I ever saw! When do we have tea?'

'As soon as you've washed your hands,' said Mrs Arnold. 'I'll get the toast and scones brought in now, so don't be long.'

They weren't long. All five of them tore upstairs,

laughing and shouting, glad to be together again. Prince Paul was pleased too – he loved this English family, with its friendliness and generosity.

When they came down, someone else was with Mrs Arnold. The three boys smiled at the small, grey-eyed woman sitting beside Mrs Arnold.

'Dimmy!' they said, and went to shake hands. Paul, as usual, bowed from his waist, and then unexpectedly gave the little woman a hug.

Dimmy's real name was Miss Dimity, and she often came to help Mrs Arnold, especially when the children were home. They all liked her, and teased her – and although she looked so gentle and timid, she could be very firm indeed, as they had found out many a time.

'Good old Dimmy!' said Mike, and looked as if he was going to try to lift her up. She pushed him off.

'No, no, Mike – I know you're almost as big as I am now – but I'm really not going to be tossed about like a bag of potatoes! Sit down before the toast gets cold.'

For a little while there was silence as the five children helped themselves from the full plates on the table. Paul gave a loud sigh.

'Now this is what I call *real* food – almost as good as Baronia. Mrs Arnold, I have been half-starved all the term!'

'Don't you believe it!' said Jack. 'You should just see the whopping great parcels he gets from Baronia every week!'

'I can guess what they are like,' said Mrs Arnold. 'Paul's mother often sends me one too – full of the most delicious things. I had a letter from the Queen, your mother, this morning, Paul. She sends you her love and is looking forward to seeing you.'

'Oh – is Paul going to Baronia very soon?' asked Nora, in a disappointed voice. 'Peggy and I haven't seen him for a whole term. Can't he stay with us for a bit?'

'Well, I have rather a surprise for you,' said her mother, smiling round. 'Paul's father and mother have an idea that they would like to come over here for a month or two, and get to know us all better. They want to bring two of Paul's brothers, as well, so that they may know a little of England before they come over here to school.'

Don't miss the next thrilling Secret Stories adventure!

Enid Blyton®

THE SECRET STORIES

The Secret
of Moon Castle

When Peggy, Mike, Nora and
Jack find a secret to unravel,
their adventures soon begin.

Prince Paul and the
Arnold children are staying
at the remote Moon Castle.
When paintings come to
life and books start flying
off shelves, the five friends
are determined to solve the
castle's spooky mysteries.